KATHY PAGE was born in 1958, the youngest of three daughters. She went to the University of York to read English and foreign languages. After receiving her degree, she stayed on in York, becoming increasingly involved in feminism and in painting. She returned to London to find 'work that had its own satisfactions but left me free to write', and chose carpentry. Following a writing course, six of the women in the class started to meet weekly and have done so ever since. Kathy Page has published short stories in *Writing Women*, *Wild Words* and *Eve Before the Holocaust*. Her first novel, *Back in the First Person*, about the experiences of a rape victim, was published by Virago in 1986 to wide acclaim. Kathy Page lives in South London and is working on her third novel.

In this, her second novel, a gripping and compassionate story of the struggles of two women, Kathy Page superbly captures the social and political climate of Edwardian England.

THE
UNBORN DREAMS
OF
CLARA RILEY

·KATHY PAGE·

Published by Virago Press Limited 1987
41 William IV Street, London WC2N 4DB

Copyright © Kathy Page 1987

British Library Cataloguing in Publication Data

Page, Kathy
    The unborn dreams of Clara Riley.
    I. Title
    823'.914[F]   PR6066.A3/

    ISBN 0-86068-900-X
    ISBN 0-86068-901-8 pbk

Typeset by Goodfellow & Egan, Cambridge and
printed in Great Britain by
Anchor Brendon of Tiptree, Essex

For
Alex, Dallas, Chantal, Judy, Julia, and Rosanne
who kept me writing and helped in many ways

.1.

For nearly twenty years, Clara has kept a yellowing page from the *London Digest*, February the first 1888, beneath the lining paper of her knife drawer. Each time she changes the lining she sees only a blur of print and completes the task as quickly as she can. Today, however, she dries her hands, removes the cutlery and gently eases it out. She takes it to the window to read.

RILEY CASE

Clara Riley, the young married woman accused of the murder of her own baby girl, was acquitted yesterday on the grounds that her act was committed in a state of temporary postpartum derangement. Mr Henderson, counsel for the defence, spoke most eloquently and movingly on her behalf, describing her as: 'a respectable, honest and hard-working married woman of the lower class, not in the least inclined towards drink or any other vice. Indeed, the very type of woman we would seek to hold up as an example to her class. Would this woman, I ask you, commit cold-blooded murder of her own issue?'

All those years ago that speech, spoken carefully, without passion but somehow hinting at it, had made something catch in Clara's chest and she'd wept a little, more from a feeling of isolation and misunderstanding (this must be the truth but it pushed her away) than from self-pity. She had to lower her eyes and wait till it was said and done.

*

'Impossible, gentlemen, you must concede. The terrible act that took place was utterly without motive of shame or financial gain such as is the common explanation in such sorry affairs. Mrs Riley made no attempt to conceal the birth of her child or her subsequent act: on the contrary she gave herself up the morning after. There can be no other explanation of her behaviour than that offered by our expert medical witness: in short, madness. Gentlemen, it is as evident that the woman who testified to this court is not mad as it is evident that she is not vicious. Gentlemen, you have heard that most women are, to a greater or lesser extent, incapacitated both physically and mentally after giving birth. The womb, that "second heart", as it might almost be called by virtue of its powerful effects on the health and emotions of the female sex, is both woman's blessing in that it enables her fulfilment in maternity, and also her bane, in that even in an otherwise healthy woman it regularly incapacitates her, particularly if she is, as I think you have seen Clara Riley to be, a woman of delicate emotions. It has indeed been said without exaggeration that women are by nature invalids for much of their lives. At regular intervals, gentlemen, disturbances called the menses proceeding from the womb reach a crisis, it is unnecessary to say more of this at this stage, and we must spare the modesty of the ladies present. How much greater the crisis is likely to be, gentlemen, after a woman has brought forth a child in hours of painful labour is a matter of common sense, but not only of common sense, for medical science has classified this particular form of hysteria – "postpartum hysteria" – as one of the gravest, yet also one of the most common and one of the most transitory, forms of mental disturbance emanating from that which makes a woman what she is . . . I ask you, would it be just to convict of murder this woman who for a few hours was overtaken by postpartum hysteria and in that state committed an act that she will regret for the rest of her life? What kind of justice would it be that punished a woman for crimes arising out of the weakness of her own biological constitution? I ask you to consider this question very carefully and humanely, for I can assure you, with the full authority of Dr Jameson and others of

2

his calibre and reputation, that this sad fate could befall any woman, and although the fashion is for nursemaids, it could as well be a woman of your own acquaintance standing here as Clara Riley.'

The jury returned a verdict of not guilty after fifteen minutes. There has been a growing reluctance to convict women brought to court on such charges. The Digest, while wary of leniency, cannot but approve the charity and sympathy shown by the jurors in this particular case where, as counsel so ably pointed out, an act of motiveless violence that went against all maternal and womanly instinct was so obviously perpetrated by a woman through no fault of her own and not in her right mind. It is to the credit of Mrs Riley's lady benefactor, whoever she may be, that Mrs Riley was represented by such able and articulate counsel as Mr Henderson.

Mrs Riley left the court with her husband Michael Riley, a carpenter's labourer, both appearing pale and silent after their ordeal, she in tears.

The tears were for Michael, not for herself. A man bound in marriage to the murderer of his child, shamed before his God, priest and the whole parish. They had to move away to hide from whiplash tongues and eyes dark with the Lord's judgement; they had to keep to themselves, and afterwards nothing was ever the same again, although of course she's used to it now. Her 'lady benefactor' Mrs Audley Jones still pays her every week for washing and ironing, and gives her a Christmas box every year. Sometimes she invites confidences, and offers herself as something approaching a friend, but this is against Clara's instincts and will. She prefers to keep herself separate. Out of politeness she used to accept from Mrs Audley Jones pamphlets about the emancipation of women, and handbills announcing public meetings: suffrage, property, divorce – she glanced at the words then used the papers as spills to light candles from the stove. Eventually she was given no more. To be able to refuse something offered was a pleasure and a luxury in itself; but now her lady benefactor has offered her help again, and she's not sure she can refuse, not sure at all.

*

All morning Clara carries baskets and tubs between the scalding steam indoors and the cruel, heartseeking wind out back: first the sweats and then the shivers. Around the copper, pans and kettles for extra water boil furiously, their handles swaddled in towelling and string. Clara's never still; grating soap, twisting, splashing, wringing, fumbling in the yard with gypsy pegs that splinter if her numbed fingers jab them too hard on to the line, she moves from one task to another without pause. To be free for bending she's left off her corsets. Her apron and dress are wet through. Maybe she's imagining it, but she feels the wet cloth sticking to the top of a tiny curve that wasn't there the month before.

This morning the wind seems to change a thousand times, confusing the criss-cross lines of white slapping and tangling in the narrow yard. She has to decide, this way or that, yes or no. Already her monthly blood comes less regularly and seems sparse. She's thirty-eight and has borne two children, easy births. The first, a son born in secret before she married, she left outside a big house in Clapham: that had been harder, strangely enough, than what she had to do to the girl . . . Oh why dredge it all up, it wasn't her fault, it wasn't really Michael's: it was the only bad thing about him, religion. That big red Pope richer than the King of England telling the poor to breed. It wasn't common sense, any more than that catechism she'd had to learn before the wedding, mumbling it time and time again, or the idea of saying what you'd done wrong in a dark cupboard while a stranger listened on the other side. If it wasn't for the Church, there were things you could do now . . .

Sleeping the girl had been, five days old and the first time she slept. It had been almost easy, but afterwards was bad because there could be no comfort, no saying, as with the boy, that she'd be well looked after, better than she could be with the life they led from hand to mouth. And if she'd been religious she could have thought of golden glowing halos, white lace froth of innocence in the heavens above. But she wasn't, she went to church when she had to and mouthed the words, but not all the King's men will ever make her swallow it, nor make her believe those crumbs dry as sawdust are real comfort or the body of anyone who ever lived, or that purple stuff is even wine, let alone blood. So afterwards there was nothing to hide what she'd done, and she was lonely because it was something all hers, like a responsibility.

She'd not tried to hide it, never; though true, she did shrink from some of its names: those the neighbours whispered, then shouted. And she'd not felt like a criminal, not even in court. Infanticide was the name of it, not murder, and Mr Henderson said it was its own punishment and later the jury said she wasn't guilty. Then there was the question of whether she was mad or not, and some said she must have been at the time, but no one said she was after. It just seemed there was nothing else she could do.

It grows dark early in the yard, being November, sheets and shirts flapping like ghosts.

But that's the past. What if now, after all these years, she takes the money from Mrs Audley Jones and does what she says? 'Termination' Mrs Audley Jones said it was called, abortion's the other word. Having your insides pulled out in someone's filthy kitchen. One of the women in the Buildings died of that she remembers, Mrs Bennet who'd earlier spat at her in the street, 'filthy murderers go to hell, even if they have friends in high places' was what she'd said. Bled to death in a pool of gin. The other woman disappeared.

'Clara,' Mrs Audley Jones said, almost a week ago now, 'something's on your mind and I think I know what it is – '

Clara froze. It wasn't on her mind but tucked far away in the back of it: it might not be true, it might not happen, it might be all right even if it did. She glared at Mrs Audley Jones then looked away. But the voice persisted, working with careful little stabs:

'You are worried, aren't you?'

'Do you think you might be expecting?'

'Is that it? Clara?'

Until Clara nodded, the backs of her eyes stretching and aching but she wouldn't cry, not if it cost her every bit of strength she had. Mrs Audley Jones rose from her chair to draw the heavy velvet curtains. There was a thick fog outside, and everything was deadly still.

'I will help you if you want. I know of a doctor who performs terminations under proper conditions and with very little risk. If you want. You can trust me, I promise. There's always a way out.'

'If you want.' It'll be, probably, her last time and chance to have a child, and they're not so poor these last years since Michael has had regular work. It would bring Michael happiness, and make amends for the past. If she gets rid of it, she'll grow old after three pregnancies but without a single child, and Michael like as not will die before she does, and so she'll be all alone and no part of her to pay its debts and beg for her memories – but hell, such memories you couldn't tell a child in any case. And with the girl, being married, she'd thought it would be different, but it wasn't: married or not she couldn't have a child, couldn't. Then it would be better to take the offer. As Mrs Audley Jones said, it wouldn't be so bad, having the operation, it would be a secret.

He'd not forgive her if he found out, never. Not again.

They'd walked home from the court in silence, her tears drying in the thin sunshine. She felt stiff and cool and empty, almost weightless. They climbed the stairs of the Buildings, right at the top they lived, and the silence seemed to grow and grow the higher they got. She watched him from behind as he struggled with the lock, no curses, still silence, the door closed carefully behind.

'Do we owe anything on the rent?' he said first. 'We'll have to go,' but he didn't wait for an answer.

6

'It's man's justice I've seen today, not God's,' he said. In those days his hair was a coppery colour, and the tears about to break made his eyes glitter in the unlit room.

'Unnatural – ungodly – you and that Henderson are the work of the devil,' he shouted, and the tears broke. Clara held herself still, she could not answer. She did not understand God, nor respect him.

'Kneel and pray for forgiveness,' he shouted, his voice ringing, and drew himself up straight. But his face quivered, and his eyes slid away from hers, and anyway, she couldn't. Behind her, something scuttled under the table. As she turned to look, he struck her, two or three times. She felt the blows pound home and her feet root themselves to the ground and she thought 'I'm stronger than he is.' Michael dropped to his knees.

'My child,' he began quietly, 'there's plenty have six or seven in circumstances far worse than ours. I don't understand, Clara, why? In all other ways you're a good woman. I don't believe this temporary madness but what else can it be? Oh Clara, it wasn't wilful murder if it was madness, what else can it be that makes a woman – why?'

Why? Clara stretched her mind to find an answer, but all that came was that feeling again, an awful desperateness that could have no other outcome. Why, why? Temporary madness was what Mr Henderson had offered, but it didn't explain, not why. Clara took Michael's arm and tried to get him to stand up.

'Perhaps I did it out of a kind of love,' she said hesitantly. 'No child should live in a world like this. Look, what could we expect for it but misery?' And as she spoke she looked around the room, almost completely dark now, but the ugliness of it still showed and she could see again the child in its box by the guttering fire, lying there bright as Christmas between four damp walls and the flaking ceiling it would have to live beneath – and her words seemed for a second to be true. Michael's eyes met hers for a long time before turning away. He shook his head.

'Perhaps – ' said Clara, and then the hopelessness of

7

explaining stopped her tongue. She felt utterly alone. What could he imagine, him with his body and life so different? The truth is, she didn't understand herself.

'Clara,' said Michael, 'I will pray for your forgiveness and I will pray to forgive you'; he no longer looked at her while he spoke, 'you are my wife and the Lord sent you to me. All suffering has a purpose.'

Later, he asked her to go to mass, but she could not say yes, and he went alone.

Michael never described to her the means whereby he forgave, if he had. There were weeks of prayer and silence, nights of weeping, and once he woke her talking, to himself it seemed, his eyes wide open but not awake.

'I cannot be one in the flesh with her until she has absolved herself, oh Lord, forgive me I cannot.'

Since then, though he might take her in his arms at night, he'd only put it in her a few times, so in a way she'd beat that red silk Vatican monkey twice over. His picture there on the wall above the sink dripping from the steam, fading like a picture on a grave.

It would be different to do it before the birth. No hint of an excuse lurking in the shadows, no postpartum hysteria, temporary madness to name if not explain: it'd be on purpose, a decision made beforehand in the light of memory. Better, as Mrs Audley Jones said, and worse: unforgivable.

In a way, it had been true about the world being no place for a child, true enough, but not why. It was something she'd thought of afterwards, but not what made her do it. Part of why was how a baby's cry got inside you, grew till you were screaming inside as well, unwilling screaming: it was as if you were an echo somehow bigger than the sound that started you off. She remembered it from her mother's last child, everyone seemed deaf to it but her. It was sick and cried all the time, died before the year was out. And her own child's cry grew

8

and grew, in the middle of the day, in the middle of the night, winding down and up the scales of pain and protest, complaining of things it hadn't even suffered yet, but *she* had and yet there was no licence for her to scream. She hadn't wept for years. And oh, that brief gasp of silence when she prayed to the God she didn't believe in that it would stop, if it did then she truly would believe; and even worse it was when she stood or paced the room with the sound, the wound clasped to her chest, when for seconds it ran through her like lightning and she wanted to run out in to the street, but couldn't. And it had seemed that it would go on for days, months, years, forever. She would be there, listening, powerless, washing away the broken bits after daylong storms, washing with suds-dulled water, grit at the bottom of the pail, nothing ever finished.

She thought that the pleasure people get from children is in the future mights and hopes and wishes, but all she could think of was the present, and it seemed the baby's wheezy breath hinted at screaming even when she finally slept, and so her own breath was held, stifling: what does she want? What does she want? She wouldn't breathe free so long as the baby did.

When she killed their child, she was at that stage of exhaustion when senseless phrases once spoken or overheard or invented repeat themselves incessantly in the head: they surfaced time and time again only minutes after she'd suppressed them. 'Over by Christmas, over by Christmas.' She finished cleaning the stove. Michael was already asleep at the other side of the room, out of reach of the pallid arc of the gaslight. Over by Christmas. Three yards of the cornflower blue . . . the baby for the first time quiet. She set her in her box in front of the stove, to get the last of the heat. Cornflower blue. Clara's body was completely limp. She leant against the table, her hands pressing down on to it, one on either side. Two sides to the square sink and the shelves either side for pans, scoured and stacked upside down. No charity ladies would come there and tell her how to keep a clean house, nor how to cook come to that. Above the sink the window covered by a gingham curtain, starting and quivering from the night-time draughts. From the other end of the table two mean steps to the bed. All these cheap rooms are the same.

The coals shrink and shift in the stove grate. She thinks she must wrap the tap down in the yard in case of freezing. She can hear Michael's breathing and the baby's, but not her own. She feels herself borne up and held immobile by a sadness that has quietly filled the little room like drifts of snow blown in through an open door. She shuts her eyes and sees bleached linen rippling slowly on the lines outside. Hopeless, hopeless.

The baby is sleeping on her back. She takes the blanket and pulls it over her face, tucking it in under the sides and top of the mattress. Where her mouth is there's a dim hollow, a small oval of thin blanket that rises and falls with her breath. Clara takes the heavy horsehair cushion from the chair and covers the moving place with it, then turns her back, listening. The sounds are like those of a bird trapped in a faraway attic, a flapping in the dark; she winces. If it doesn't finish soon she will not be able to bear it, this child that screamed as if it was being murdered for the first hours of her life now scarcely able to muster a sound, the noise of tiny struggles but no breath, and then it slows to nothing, no sound, no breath, no movement from the box behind her back; and suddenly Clara hears her own breath mingling with Michael's from the other side of the room, long and slow it is, in and a pause then out, like waves on the sea. Without turning back to look in the box, she walks round the table to the bed, lies down dressed on top of the covers and takes to desperate sleep. Her breath growing greedy and heavy as if oblivion were a battle or a lover, she goes into it fighting, for life, for breath, for sleep itself.

Cornflower blue.

It wasn't, she had known it mustn't be, an act of violence. She'd not done it when she most wanted to, when all her muscles ached and yearned for the swift gesture that would extinguish. Waking early she walked straight from the bed to the door and told the first constable she met what she had done in the night.

The wind outside blows steadier now, and Clara's muscles have gone beyond fatigue; she carries the heaped baskets unaware, folds and piles and begins again.

Her first child, a boy, slid secret from her flesh at four in the morning. She remembers the agony of not being able to make a sound, and how she gave it brandy straight away so no one would hear. She kept him four days before leaving him.

It was the tail end of autumn, smelling of mould and chimneys; it was damp and cold and she felt colder still inside because of the steely twistings of envy which always came to her, like headaches after drink, when she walked past those big gabled houses prinked with velvet, satin and brass. She was pierced and chilled with hating what she could not have, with wanting it. The child would have it, she thought – it was a kind of revenge in its way.

Clara sat on the wrought iron seat where the Avenue and the Crescent crossed, feeling aches in the stringy blue veins that had come on her thighs and calves like crazing on a plate. The baby – no point really in a name, though sometimes she caught herself thinking of him as William – slept in his carefully folded piece of blanket, thin streams of spume linking his nostrils and upper lip, looking like someone very old or a bit simple. She cleaned his face, very gently, so as not to disturb him. The sugared milk and water he'd had before they set out was thin and soon he'd be awake, screaming his emptiness, twisting her up inside with different things at once.

She looked up at the houses opposite: it didn't really matter which. She chose the one where the tradesman's entrance was completely hidden by a laurel hedge, but then, no, it would be better, and safer even, to go up the wide marble steps bold as brass to the panelled front door . . .. thinking this frightened her, the door forbade, the windows were eyes.

Then, they were lighting the gas. The dusk there in the tree-lined avenue was thick and richer than in the streets a mile away. Invisible hands slid the curtains across: she could almost feel the warmth inside, smell the brandy-soaked fruit and marzipan of winter cakes. She shivered. Their sons would rape you, and then they'd throw you out when you got a child, call you a lying whore: but sticky with hymn-book charity and smelling of cologne they would, she thought, take her son and unwrap him and bathe him and put him in white towels. They would see him all right. She couldn't. Leave it where it damn well came from.

A bastard, born 'out of wedlock'. They would imagine her with scorn. She walked to the porch, glancing rapidly between the patch of light at the top of the steps and the baby's shadowy face; he looked young again then.

'Goodbye then, you,' she muttered, thinking: he won't remember except perhaps in a dream.

'You make sure they treat you decent, you give them hell and put on some fat.' She felt nothing except fear in case someone opened the door or parted the curtains to look out into the night. She laid him right in front of the door, where he couldn't be missed. There was a pounding in her ears. 'Don't scream, don't scream,' she willed at him, 'don't scream, you bastard.' She couldn't run for fear her shoes would make too much noise; with each step the damp gravel shifted with a sound like the breaking of tiny bones. At the end of the avenue where Lil was waiting she stopped to listen, imagining a cry. But there was none. She could see her breath in the air. They began to run, arm in arm.

Her first thought had been to leave it with the Rosenburys at Western Crescent. That was where it came from, but then, that would make them less likely to take it. It was Marcus Rosenbury's, he was the eldest son. He came in when she was sitting resting on his bed in the middle of cleaning his room. She was embarrassed and frightened he'd be angry at the liberty taken, but, 'Oh no,' he said, 'don't worry at all, I'll just

sit here by you, you rest your feet. What is it they call you?'
'Clara. Blue eyes you have, Clara, cornflower blue eyes . . .'
kissed her and pushed her back on the bed, lay next to her and
ran his hands up and down her body. 'Don't – you – worry,
don't – you – worry', like he was talking to an animal, calming
a horse, but it worked; she lay tense but not struggling, his
hand resting where her legs met her body. 'Don't tell anyone,'
he said. Pressure, just below where freedom of movement
stopped, her upper body suddenly pulled tight with metal
stays, hand just lying there, but heavy, heavier than an
accidental hand would be. She felt weak and dizzy, couldn't
breathe – of course she wouldn't tell, who could she tell?
What words were there? Who would believe her? The power
of that hand: it was drawing all her breath and blood where it
pressed, she swallowed, her mouth filled again. She was
sixteen years old. He smiled at her, repeated, 'Promise you
won't tell, blue eyes.' She swallowed again, still dumb,
nodded.

'Come here the same time tomorrow,' he whispered, laughed,
then got up and left the room. She went straight back to
cleaning the grate, her eyes out of focus. Filthy work, Clara
remembers, her hands now immersed in soapy water for the
hundredth time today. However much they hurt at least
they're clean now. The dry cinders were light and fragile but
they could still make you bleed, they sucked the water out of
you. She didn't know what to think, but in any case she had
to be there the day after to clean the room as usual; had she
liked what he did yesterday, she wondered, and couldn't
answer: there was something awful in the weakness it put her
in. But that second time she knew she didn't like it – he did it
with his hand over her mouth. His hand smelled of soap. For a
minute it felt guilty-good, the sharp coldness of the shuttered
room on the tops of her legs, but she was frightened by the
silence and his way of breathing like he was in a fight: she
screwed her eyes shut and she realised her face was all twisted
away as though someone was about to slap her. She didn't
know what else to expect; the feeling didn't come back like

13

yesterday and then there was something jabbing at her. He swore, breath biting in and out between his teeth, pushed her leg aside, and then came the pain, oh yes he must have known, that's why he covered her mouth, and now he didn't need to remind her not to tell because she knew it wasn't a thing a girl was meant to do and she didn't want it done again; but then, he said he'd tell if she didn't.

As the weeks went by it hurt less. Nearly every other day, with the early-morning house quiet about them, Clara lay there doing what she knew was wrong, but then it didn't seem to matter much. Less and less was said; Marcus Rosenbury's face, long and sullen but just beginning to flesh out, would twist into a kind of sneer then turn abruptly away from her as if something had happened to it that she must not see, and it was over. Pig ignorant she was, she'd not put two and two together and what chance had she, what chance for it not to happen? She didn't know a thing. Thinking back makes her angry at her own stupidity and at being used by the Rosenburys: a thin girl she was, and the work seemed as hard as being down the mines. They had no mercy and they liked you to twitch a tiny smile – not too much, for that was disrespectful – when you took your orders.

'Clara, you're going to have a baby, ain't you? What are you going to do? They'll give you notice and how'll you be able to feed it?' said her friend Lil. She can remember it like a picture. It was Sunday afternoon in the park, the same park they'd met in over a year before. Straight lines of tulips marching into the distance on beds fringed with blue, dry brown grass and a line of trees shimmering where the lake was. She turned to Lil, who wore a new hat with paper flowers on, shocked, but already realising. Lil stopped walking.

'I thought we were going for a boat ride,' Clara said.

'Come on, who was it?' asked Lil, 'I wasn't born yesterday even if you were.'

'Marcus Rosenbury.'

14

Lil let her breath out between her teeth and they started walking again.

'Have they said anything, your people?'

'No.'

'They will, my girl, they will. What are you going to do? . . . You've got to twist their arm, that's what you've got to do! You must tell Mrs Rosenbury who it was and that he must marry you. He won't of course, but they'll pay you off, see, in case you talk. That's what you do.'

Lil sealed her lips and handed over the threepence for the boat ride. They sat together in silence, watching the dark green water and the startled ducks. Neither of them really believed it would work.

'They found a young girl here last month,' said Lil, 'in your condition. You don't want to do anything silly like that. After all, you've got a friend.'

No doubt because he saw what Lil saw, Marcus Rosenbury stopped coming about that time. And because the cause was removed, it made it all the easier to believe that it wasn't happening. As each day went by the worry slowly melted, like a shirt stiff with frost brought in to dry by the fire. Everything returned to normal, as if none of it had ever been. The way Lil looked at her made her uneasy and she avoided her three Sundays in a row. She loosened her stays yet managed not to notice that her belly was inching outwards, or if she did, she perhaps believed that now the morning visits had stopped it would somehow begin to shrink and flatten – all she had to do was wait. She polished the brass and smiled at the strange reflected face looming yellow and goblin-like. At least she found bearable the work that had seemed impossibly hard before. In the evenings she crept down to the kitchen for bread and dripping, thick-smeared with brown jelly.

Mrs Rosenbury sent for her. She said only, 'Clara, I'm giving you a week's notice.'

And Clara said, 'But why, Ma'am?'

'I don't know how you have the face to ask.' Mrs Rosenbury's eyes descended slowly to her belly, returned, almost it seemed amused, to her face. To twist her arm was as impossible as to beg for time.

Clara threw away the gift of baby clothes parcelled in new brown paper. She didn't want their gifts. Marcus Rosenbury was their only son, and those little blue nightdresses, softer than any cloth she'd ever worn, must have been his. And of course, Mrs Rosenbury must have guessed. Lil tried to persuade her to go back and ask for money, but it all seemed too late, and by then she'd thought of the idea: first it was to leave the child on their back step with a note: 'Marcus's child, look after me', but then she realised it would be better to choose a house she didn't know, and leave it with no explanation.

There wasn't much work for a maid with no references and none at all for one with a belly like hers. Lil said lie low, and brought her sewing work: cuffs for gentlemen's shirts, and stacks of cards that needed folding and pairing with envelopes in different shades of white. And she brought cold potatoes and cheese when she could take them from where she worked. Clara grew pale from staying indoors in the tiny room with its window so high you couldn't reach to clean it, but she took Lil's advice: stood then squatted twenty times morning and night, though sometimes that too made the room shimmer and swim before her eyes. Lil gave her a long, hard look when she told her what she intended to do with the child.

'You might find it harder to do than it is to say,' she remarked, 'you might find you've come to feel for it, probably will.'

Clara, sitting on the table with her back resting on the wall, stabbed at the stiff white cloth she was sewing.

'I never wanted any of it,' she said. She wanted to make some violent movement, but the weight of her stomach seemed to press her back against the wall. It was too dark to see the stitches she was making. The room was so small that the two of them seemed to fill it entirely.

'I know,' said Lil quietly. 'It's a good idea and if that's what you want to do when the time comes, I'll help you. We'll go for a walk, eh, when it gets to be really dark.'

When it came to it, Lil walked to the end of the Avenue with her and waited. The birth hadn't been hard, neither of them had been hard. The priest that Michael sent to visit her in the Buildings told her that God said a woman shall give birth in pain and suffering, so much as to say, you can't complain, you can't refuse. But there'd been little pain. She was large-hipped, despite being thin, built for it you might say. It's not giving birth that's hard, she thinks, wringing sheets into the square sink, it's afterwards. Dear Lil, bit of a friend, bit of a mother. Sometimes she seemed so much older than me, though she wasn't, and sometimes it was as if she admired me. You couldn't have a friend better than her. She was small, with shiny patches where the bones of her face pushed under the surface of her skin. Came from the West Country, with cheeks red as apples, Lil.

Once, she went with a man for dinner and somewhere to stay. She was a whole year older and wiser: she kept her eyes wide open and in the half dark saw what she'd only felt before. Remembered her mother's bittersweet laughter, washing a baby boy. But her mother liked babies, though it was having them that killed her . . . Now this could make her have one again, but it was a chance she had to take, that thrust itself upon her because of the fear that hunger brings. Sometimes you're all right, she thought. She'd had bad luck before, but this time she'd escape and she washed herself inside afterwards, washed and washed. Lil was sick and there was nothing else she could think to do: it must have been 1886, there was little work even for the strong. The man was generous enough, call-me-Henry, his eyes swimming bright and his breath smelled catch-your-throat-sweet of spirits, but he talked without slurring and gave her some money; almost proud she felt. But she'd not felt, then or ever since that first time when Marcus Rosenbury's hand lay on her there (don't you tell anyone, don't tell), she'd not felt that rising feeling, that power.

'Who could I tell, who could I tell?' she thinks, now as then.

She'd used the man's money to buy a bottle of tonic for Lil, and some thick cream and malt bread. But when she went to the house to ask of her they said she'd had the doctor but died all the same.

She didn't miss the next month, though. She was all right.

Clara wrings the last sheet and takes it into the yard, feeling in the dark for the line. Michael will be home soon. There's no moon but the clouds are all silvery, lit from behind. She watches them until the cold and her wet clothes make her shiver. Her mind's not made up. Thinking of the past has left her with a kind of sadness that's almost calm.

Michael's hands are scrubbed clean, his nails cut and dug out so that neat crescents of white scallop the ends of his fingers, like fringes on upholstery or fancy curtains. But for the number of scars and the hardness of the skin inside they are more like a clerk's hands than those of a carpenter's labourer. He holds them now, clasped on the deal table that he made, knuckles as neatly interlocked as the dovetail joints on the knife-drawer. His eyes are shut above the steam rising from his soup, his moustache and lashes are pale, the skin of his face mottled with freckles fading in the winter dark. His ginger hair is bleaching and thinning, dusty looking.

'Bless us our Lord and these thy gifts . . .' he begins, and Clara, not eating but not praying either, looks at his closed eyelids and tries the thought: 'I am going to deceive him.' She can't remember that she's concealed anything from him since they were married, though she has her secrets about the time before. She could never have told him about the boy left in the Avenue, how could she have? He wanted to save her from falling into vice: how could she have said she'd already fallen? He wouldn't have wanted her then. He was her friend after Lil died, he married her when there was no work to speak of, when she was so thin she looked ten years past her age; he undertook to save her from hunger and ruin and loneliness, to cleave to her and no other; he's never deceived her, never done anything she could complain of . . .

'Amen.' She joins Michael in that for form's sake and because it seems worth winking at the God that commands forgiveness, forbids the sundering of marriage ties and created limbo for the unbaptized child. She owes Him that much at least.

'Amen.' Michael smiles, falling on his meal.

'I've got more work with Mr Holden,' he says, 'enough to last past Christmas, but the pay's less than before.' He eats fast but cleanly, holding his full spoon a second over his plate for the drips to slide back, using a knife to break his bread. His pale blue eyes follow the movements of his own hands and intermittently those of Clara's hands and lips.

'It may not be much but it's better than nothing,' he reflects, examining the neat cast his teeth have cut into the cheese. After all these years their meal together is something of a daily pleasure to him, not just for the food. He takes exactly half the cheese she's set out, and pushes the rest to her.

'There's plenty of men,' Clara says, 'that take the savoury things all to themselves.'

'I like to be fair. I'm content with what I have,' Michael says, smiling. 'I'm not,' Clara thinks sharply. But it's true he would make a good father, fair. He doesn't drink. Twisted-sad it is that he should be paired with her, so bad at mothering . . . while other women bear packs of brats to such men as should've been stopped from breeding.

'Mr Holden calls me his mate, but he keeps my money at less than half of what the trade gets, and I can do work as good as his, if he'd let me,' says Michael, his voice devoid of bitterness, perplexed rather.

'I can't,' Clara gasps inside.

'Is something the matter?' He's staring at her, reminding her for a second of those portraits: chalky, stuffy-looking people but the eyes, oh how shiny and alive-looking the eyes were: she used to feel those painted eyes burning into her back

as she cleaned the Rosenburys' reception room. They would
see if she missed anything.

'I was thinking how good you've been to me, that's all.'

'I do what I can,' he says, filling his mouth and chewing
more slowly than usual. 'The past is a cross I must bear. The
Lord doesn't send suffering without reason or hope. No man
has the right to say he has been dealt more than he can bear.'

His words seem a judgement on her, and something in her
hardens against him. He cares more for God than anything on
this earth, she thinks. Michael's face has softened.

'But you know, Clara, I sometimes wish life wasn't so
hard . . . if I'd been able to do my time and get trade rates,
we'd be living elsewhere, and you'd not have to work. Mr
Holden's wife even has a maid. Perhaps then – '

'If we lived somewhere else, the rent would be more,' she
interrupts, not liking spoken dreams, not liking the brokenness
of his words, the maudlin-jump-in-the-heartbeat, the impossibility of them: she wants to force them back down his throat,
to smother them, and stifle any further reference to what he
called 'the past'. The past has lain between them, forgotten,
forgiven or perhaps only sleeping, for nearly twenty years.
Tonight it seems to have invaded the air Clara breathes, to
live briefly in her blood as she inhales, to fade but not quite
die as the air slips away between her lips. It is as if she were
two people.

Michael bangs his pipe smartly on the table, coughs. Soon
they will both be tired. The air in the room is still thick from
all the day's boiling of water and of soup; half-dry shirts and
sheets wait in piles for their turn to perch on racks by the fire.
The room is never dry except sometimes at the very height of
summer. In the morning the windows will seem as if they have
been weeping in the night.

Clara stands up, a big woman though thin, taller and
broader than her husband, stronger too. Michael was turned
down for the army, even when they took any kind of weakling.
They never said why. There are days when he can scarcely get
his breath: the lingering steam sogs up his lungs and opening

20

the window only makes it worse. She'd thought it might be consumption, but if it had been he'd be dead by now; perhaps it was the sawdust and plaster at work. She's never been sick that she can remember; even when near-starved her cheeks though hollow were pink, her eyes brighter than usual. She carries five-gallon tubs and wrestles with lines of fighting cloth taut as sails in the gusty winds that bolt panic-stricken down their dead end of a street. But now she feels feeble, almost dizzy, the cups and bowls overburden her as she carries them to the sink.

'I can't do it,' she says to herself several times, trying the sound of it. But it's complicated: she doesn't quite know if she means she can't hide it from him, or do it to him, or if she can't have it done to her, or can't raise a child; she would like not to have to do any of these things but must choose between them.

'Your work's longer than mine,' Michael says suddenly, making her start. He sits awkward at the table, not sure where he can go to be out of her way, watching to see if she will be washing the dishes or ironing. If they had a child, she thinks, it would perhaps earn enough for the times when he couldn't get work, or she lost customers. Another wage, but another person too, and then a girl would make less than it took to feed her.

'If we got another iron, I could help you sometimes of an evening,' he says, turning the lamp up.

'Oh no,' Clara says, close to the tears that would betray her and mislead him, 'you do too much.'

Michael is not a particularly vain man, but gratitude warms his heart, and almost always tears, guilt, pain, despair will soften it.

They lie together in bed; she thinks he is asleep. Beneath her under-petticoat her hands rest on her belly, feeling again. There's no doubt it's a child; that forced outness is tight and full, comes from within. She can see the piles of ironed whites making glimmering ghost shapes in the room. Experimentally she puts her hand where Marcus Rosenbury's once pushed and pushes as he did. Tears come to her eyes from some nameless pain. How can it be a sin and a temptation? Why did Michael tell her on her wedding night that she ought to follow him and pray after for forgiveness, ask that the so-called pleasure, sung of in music palaces, overheard in other women's laughter, wouldn't count against her in the life to come? A sin to let him perhaps. But marriage was blessed by the Church: go forth and multiply, bless the little children. Once married, a man had a right to. Something's missing in me, she thinks and pushes harder: nothing, only pressure and the beginnings of pain. And none of the babies that came from there could be held with love. It seems they've brought her nothing but cost her all, her private parts.

'Don't cry,' Michael says softly. 'We'll be all right. We'll have a proper bird this Christmas, and then in the new year, – Clara, do you realise it'll be 1910?' He pauses momentarily, caught in the amazement of passing time, feeling it as quick and visible as sand running through the narrow neck of an hour glass.

'In the new year, who knows what the good Lord will bring . . .' Clara feels the hand she's holding try to pull away: his instinct, she knows, is to cross himself when talking of the unknown, but she doesn't release him and instead he takes her other hand and squeezes it, two pressures now forcing the salt water out of her like she was a blister ready to burst. 'I'm lonely,' she thinks, 'lonely making my mind up like this.'

Clara carries the wrapped laundry round to Mrs Audley Jones, sheets and blouses and shirts and the best tablecloths. She used to get collars and linen to starch as well, but now they go to the steam laundry. She's lucky they don't take the lot away from her. It's either because Mrs Audley Jones is sorry for her or because her work is that bit better than what they get from the laundry. Clara's work is meticulous, even on the days when she hates it.

A skinny little girl is stooping to pick up russet-and-cox-coloured autumn leaves blown into the street. She stands up as Clara passes.

'Got a hapenny, missus?' she asks, and holds the leaves out to her. 'I've got no one in the world.' Her arms and legs are dirty, her eyes fixed steadily on Clara's face; impossible to tell if what she says is lies or truth. Clara feels in her pocket, but there's nothing there.

'No,' she says, walking away as fast as she can. The leaves were beautiful: collecting them was the sort of thing she would have done as a child. Her elder brothers were twins, both serving on ships; they came home with bits of lace and silk and little wooden animals, and then they drowned at sea. It was bad luck for sailors to know how to swim, but they'd swum in the red-coloured river water out back since soon after they could walk. And she remembers her sister Vicky washing and combing her hair for her when she was small. Vicky declared you couldn't breathe, you couldn't breathe in England (though she'd only ever seen Sheffield really), and so she set sail for Canada with John Davies who she'd only married because he wanted to go there as well. Letters came twice a year, then once, then not at all, so no one knew what had become of Vicky who'd combed her hair and sometimes told stories of far places she'd never seen. 'I've bred a race of wanderers,' her mother said, 'everyone goes in the end.' She'd lost her husband and half her babies as well: maybe that was why she let her last surviving, Clara, go without much fight.

'Sheffield,' she'd pleaded with her mother, 'there's nothing but steel, steel and iron, the foundry and the factory, I want a bit better – ' 'You're maybe right,' her mother answered, sounding the maybe.

When she was small, her mother used to take her out bramble picking on the hills outside town. Every year they went, and afterwards at night when she closed her eyes the black fruit had printed themselves all over the space inside her head, like printed cloth for making a dress.

Sheffield was darker even than London, dirtier too, but it was smaller and you could see the edges of it: you could imagine getting away, follow with your eyes the railway tracks snaking off into the distance. She used to run up hills to see

23

what was on the other side. There was always a shifting layer of smoke, but if she got high enough she could just see the blues and greens and purple beyond. She remembers the reddish earth in winter, and the cabbage fields that were a metallic green, quite different from the green of pastures.

The canvas bag she uses for carrying the laundry begins as always to weigh on her about half-way there; she untwists the handles from her wrists, changes hands and slows down. Now she's started to remember her family, it all seems a list of deaths, disappearance and disappointments. The people she's cared for have all been snatched away: Vicky, the twins, Lil, her mother. Furtively, she adds them to the losses she herself has brought about, reluctant somehow to admit that they are the same. Altogether it's seven. She sees them as short, black, tally marks, four slashed by a diagonal, then two more, the two that stand wilfully apart, her children that aren't. If she has the termination there will be three of those; then perhaps herself and Michael to follow, completing the second tally.

What was it Mrs Audley Jones said?

'It's not killing, no, Clara, it's far different from killing, surely you can see? The doctors call it termination, it's like cutting out a bit of you, not killing someone else. It's an operation, done before it's a proper child. Much better, Clara, than what might – '

Cutting out a bit of you. Sounds more like killing than what she did to the girl. There was no knives and blood in what I did, she thinks.

Clara usually looks forward to the twice a week when she fetches and returns laundry to Mrs Audley Jones. Always there's sweet, fresh-tasting tea and yellow cake or a piece of ham and starch-white bread with the crusts cut off, given to her by Jeanne Biggs with permission or even by order of Mrs Audley Jones. And sometimes when Mrs Audley Jones is at home she and Jeanne Biggs go up to the drawing room to eat it with her. And Clara thinks she's made to feel almost like a proper guest. She often imagines how unrecognisably different her life would be if all those years ago she'd been taken on there, instead of at the Rosenburys', how nothing, none of it would have happened. That so little a distinction between which particular house you served as maid could make such a vast difference to the outcome of your life: it was almost funny, but somewhere deep down it also made her want to curse; you were like something tossed up on the side of a river, your fate in others' hands to be wasted or used . . . the luck of the dice.

Today, she dreads Mrs Audley Jones being there and knows she will be; she'll ask Clara into the fresh, sunbathed drawing room, light bouncing gaily amongst the clutter of polished surfaces, and she'll get her alone like last week when Jeanne Biggs had left the slices of cake and tea things already set – given leave, Mrs Audley Jones said, to visit her sister. She dreads it because she hasn't made up her mind and when Mrs Audley Jones asks her what she has decided the pain of choosing will come all at once like pulling a tooth, and she'll no longer be like a guest, she'll be a silly laundry woman who can't think straight and, stammering, not know what to say.

She knows that Mrs Audley Jones is eight years older than herself, but her face, despite lines, is younger. There's a brightness about it; by comparison, her own seems half-asleep. Of course, Mrs Audley Jones's hands are perfect, white, slightly warm to the touch. From Jeanne Clara knows that she had a son born in the early years of her first marriage, grown now and died in India. Mrs Audley Jones herself rarely talks to Clara of her family or her past. She talks about the emancipation of women and the news in the papers. Votes For Women: it seems a tiny and useless thing, compared to the agonies of the present.

After that only son, Clara wonders, what happened then? Did Mrs Audley Jones herself ever have the termination operation? How did she manage with her first husband? He died when he was only forty, of a piece of something stuck in him after the war. There was no love lost. Jeanne Biggs said there were days when the bell would ring all day: 'Take this tray away, please,' one would say. 'No Jeanne, leave it,' the other. 'If looks could kill,' Jeanne said, but she always obeyed Mrs, since it was her that took her on, and her that would stand by you in the end.

Of course, people who were rich and outside the Church could use things to stop getting children. There were even ladies distributing rubber johnnies to the poor. One of them had gone to prison. Them on the one hand, the Pope on the other, you pays your money and takes your choice who tells you what to do. Mrs Audley Jones can do what she likes, money in the bank, big house, and her second husband, the Admiral, only home twice a year. His thin-faced portrait hung in the hall, but the house lived without him. Why had she married again? Of course, she wasn't always such a suffragist.

'Marriage is a woman's only career,' Mrs Audley Jones once said, 'and she loses her name and her papers and herself when she embarks upon it.'

At the back of Clara's mind indecision butts and nudges like an extra sleeper in bed, one too many gently and obstinately pushing, bringing wakefulness, exhaustion, pricking tears of rage. To stand now and sleep forever she thinks, shutting her eyes a moment before banging on the service door. She's saved: Jeanne Biggs is there after all, her tight-laced body a solid buffer, a well-fed maternal presence like a great pillar she can dodge behind to hide from that awful question, 'Well, Clara, have you decided . . .'

'You're late deary, it's gone ten and I've boiled the kettle twice. Gawd – ' Jeanne exclaims as she takes the densely packed laundry bag, 'no wonder.' She can speak coarsely and she can speak proper according to the company. The shadowy kitchen is dry and hot. Clara, feeling her face burning at the change from the raw cold outside, rubs her sore hand sheepishly.

'We're to take our bite upstairs; come on, off with that coat – if you can call it a coat.' Jeanne looks pointedly at Clara's

26

shoes; she wipes them and follows up to where the smell of cooking gives way to lavender and beeswax.

'She's not been well,' whispers Jeanne, her voice husky, caught half-way between kitchen and drawing room. 'Should be resting, I say, but no, she said she'd like to see you.' The tray quakes as she turns round to look at Clara, wide-eyed to emphasise the honour, half jealous, half pleased for Clara's sake. 'She's the type that draws people, puts herself out. She works too hard – ' continues Jeanne who, Clara knows, rises a good two hours before Mrs Audley Jones. 'Women's suffrage, Women's rights, all sorts. All over the country she goes and they'll never get it, it's been going on since before you and I were born. And what good – '

'Come by the fire,' says Mrs Audley Jones, a small voice, but it carries well, 'it's so nice to be at home.'

'Are you feeling more rested now?' asks Jeanne as she fusses with the tray. It is at Mrs Audley Jones's request that she does not use the customary 'ma'am', but at least half the time it slips out unawares.

'Thank you, I am completely recovered now,' Mrs Audley Jones pauses to stir sugar noiselessly into tea. The sugar in its rose painted bowl is as fine and white as salt. Clara and Jeanne settle themselves as quietly as possible.

'Well . . .' begins Mrs Audley Jones, and in the silence after Clara can hear all their breathing, her own catching suddenly – she's never going to ask me now, with Jeanne here? ' . . . indeed it was tiring, but worthwhile. I travelled to Manchester in a second class carriage. It was perfectly comfortable, indeed I felt more at ease than I would have otherwise . . . I never truly feel that I belong where I'm supposed to be! Even in that great hall with nearly a thousand others like me, united in opposition to one of the world's great wrongs, I felt myself as a person apart. A lesser person, but also greater . . . unable to blindly follow either a crowd or a leader – '

She's not going to ask me, Clara thinks. She can hear Jeanne's cup rattling slightly on its saucer, or is it her own?

Perhaps Mrs Audley Jones expects Clara to find some way of telling her even with Jeanne there, yes or no, a slow nod or shake of the head, nothing ever said – yes or no? It's impossible to hold her attention to what Mrs Audley Jones is saying, let alone understand it.

' . . . but how else to be united? We are divided and so weakened. One must hold with one or the other, when neither is quite right. In the end it's a matter of doing what one can, in all conscience . . . '

Mrs Audley Jones, whose face has become slack, her eyes clouded as she speaks, drains her almost cold tea with a slight shudder.

'Mrs Brett said to me, "your trouble is you're an individualist, like myself, but best keep it between these four walls, my dear, because no one will ever trust you once they know." But –' Mrs Audley Jones's eyes come sharply into focus, 'I wonder if it's not a question of cowardice above all else.' She laughs, and the cup hits its saucer with a sharp ringing sound that seems to signal the end of her reflections.

'And how on earth do you manage to dry the laundry, Clara, in weather like this?' she asks, refusing the madeira cake. 'Even with the fire raging the air still seems damp.'

'The iron,' Clara says mechanically, 'does the last bit of drying.' The butter-rich cake melts in her mouth unnoticed. Perhaps, she thinks, she's forgotten, or changed her mind and there's an end to it.

'Clara, I do believe you're shivering.' Mrs Audley Jones gathers her stole around her shoulders and stands up. 'Come upstairs with me, I have a coat that will fit you. If you would clear the things away, Jeanne . . . '

The bulk of the coat feels as if it's pushing Clara into the floor.

'Turn around,' says Mrs Audley Jones, pushing her shoulder gently, 'turn around.' Clara sees herself in the large mirror; her face, above the dark cloth and the thickness of the fox-fur collar, which surprised her at first by how cold it felt, looks flaky white and insubstantial.

'Which do you prefer?' asks Mrs Audley Jones, and Clara doesn't know, can't choose. In the corner of her eye lurks a shadow of that other question, which waits until this one is answered, so all choosing is impossible.

There is a faint smell of camphor coming from the coat.

'Jeanne won't be jealous,' says her tormentor lightly. 'She had her choice only yesterday – and quite different from either of these. Your looks are completely opposite.'

Mrs Audley Jones has never spoken like this before, never prattled about dresses or hair, complexions or jewellery. Clara has a half thought: is she as frightened as I am? Uninvited, she sits heavily on a tapestry stool.

'Myself, I think the –'

'This one,' Clara interrupts suddenly, 'so long as you are sure, Mrs Audley Jones, this is the one I'd rather have and thank you very much.'

She begins to undo the closely spaced buttons as fast as she can, proper horn they are, and one comes off in her hand. Thinking, what on earth does she think of me? she puts the tiny button straight in the pocket before it's noticed. Her face is hot. I do frighten her, yes I do. Why? She has to stand to remove the coat, and standing brings her near, suddenly only a few inches between their faces.

'Mrs Audley Jones,' she says, and the syllables seem all mixed up as if she was drunk, 'I haven't been able to make up my mind – I've thought and thought – ' There's a meeting of stricken eyes. Mrs Audley Jones's are blue and huge, the irises floating free in a sea of white. Suddenly, before Mrs Audley Jones can reply, all the arguments say themselves at once in Clara's mind: surely it's better than – you know it would be no different this time, know it in your bones; he'll never know of it, it would only make things worse; it's not a child, it's like cutting a piece out of your own body; it's secret, I can trust her; what else can I do? I can't refuse –

'But I must, I've got to have – the operation, what you said.' Clara weeps, and Mrs Audley Jones takes her into her arms; for a few seconds there's no speaking, only the crackling and shuffling of coals in the grate, and Clara's strangled sobs.

'Now it's not so terrible as that,' says Mrs Audley Jones, and she could be trying to reassure over the operation, or she could be referring to those last trapped struggles and scuffles the girl made as she died, sounds which seem now to mingle with the other quiet sounds in the room. And has she had the termination herself? Clara knows she'll never dare to ask.

'This week,' says Mrs Audley Jones, her voice low, 'I shall make all the arrangements, I shall tell you what we have to do and I shall have the money – ' There is a hint of excitement in her voice, suppressed perhaps because it would be unseemly.

She offers Clara a watery smile.

'Because of the circumstances, Clara, I think it's the only thing to do. It's something that many, many women of all classes turn to in desperation.'

Clara returns the smile, though hers is wary.

'It must be in the daytime because – '

'Of course, Clara dear – ' and Clara sinks, flounders into the warmth of Mrs Audley Jones's voice and the aftermath of her own worry and bravery and tears. She has decided, and it is for the best.

Forgetting how it fades her face, Clara leaves the house swaddled in her new coat; the old one, paper-wrapped, in one of her laundry bags. On her way to the Corner Eating House to pick up napkins and glass-cloths she does sums in her head: the week's money, hers and Michael's, less the cost of soap and bleach and gas and coal. Less the rent divided by seven, the amount for each day, less a bit to be saved – the answer comes out near nothing, all her sums seem to come out to that same answer. When, if, there's more, she will buy some cloth for shirts and blouses. 'Count your blessings. When you've learnt that you'll have learnt a good lesson none too soon,' was what her mother used to say. But everything in Clara refuses this advice; those words saying themselves in her head make her want to screw them up and spit them out. And how can a few pence in your hand be a blessing anyway. A blessing ought to be out of the ordinary, rich: a summer night not true dark but with a colour like that of very ripe damsons, easy laughter, freedom. Those would be blessings worth the counting. It's dangerous, she thinks, to regret anything, to change your mind once something was spoken or done. Reasons and causes go in layers like old dirt; dreams and wants shine like new coins in your hand.

Clara sets the whites in bowls of blueing, and picks the remains of paper off the meat she bought. So solid it looks, a heavy lump of red, once flesh; and it strikes her: this is what I'm made of. She puts her knife down as if it might leap straight up and cut her into meat. How will they get it out? Will they stick steel knives in her flesh? Sheffield steel it says on the blade. Will they cut her insides with a blade of the Sheffield steel she ran away from? 'Properly,' she hears Mrs Audley Jones's voice, saying the word carefully. 'Some of the doctors who do it for poor women aren't even doctors. The things I've heard would turn your stomach and make your blood boil, Clara, but this is a proper doctor who attends ladies and gentlemen. It will be cleanly and properly done in a proper surgery – ' Doctors are black-coated men who rush up when there's an accident, crowds parting before them. Once she saw someone run over by a train, the doctor, calm as a priest, shaking his head and brushing cinders and dust from his trouser knees.

And there was something else Mrs Audley Jones once said, about the time when the police could arrest any woman they thought might be on the game and take her to a doctor to see if she was clean or not, and lock her up in hospital if she wasn't. The prevention of contagious diseases it was called, but it was only women they took in and any fool could see that wouldn't cure it. She shudders thinking of girls lying there on slabs with their skirts up, doctors with their fingernails, clean and trimmed but still sharp: Would it be like that, her operation? All that had been stopped when she was still a girl by ladies like Mrs Audley Jones complaining, there were questions in Parliament, even so, it had taken nearly twenty years to put a stop to it. Maybe they'd still get the vote then, if they went on long enough.

'If women had had the vote,' said Mrs Audley Jones, 'laws like that would have never been passed', and laughing she added, 'And if – when – there are women in Parliament – '

How can she have such faraway, impossible-sounding hopes? She's another one like me, none too good at counting her blessings, Clara thinks, half bitter, half pleased.

Termination, like the tram's end. Putting an end to it, that's what the operation's about. Slower than usual, Clara cuts the meat into small cubes and rolls them in flour which stains pink. She rushes them to the pan of fat, smoking and spitting on the stove. In seconds they are brown and no longer flesh; she adds water and salt, they will be soft and unrecognisable in an hour or so. She will eat and forget, she will work and forget, there's no going back.

Mrs Audley Jones hands several sheets of her own handwriting to Mrs Brett, and waits while she reads.

'This is for Sunday?' Mrs Brett asks. 'You will most certainly have your knuckles rapped, I can tell you that. It's a mercy there's no sense of personal ambition behind your politics. You're going in every direction at once, aren't you?'

'Don't you think it's true?' asks Mrs Audley Jones. Mrs Brett is sitting at her large desk, her elbows firmly planted on it, her chin resting on clenched hands. Her face, beginning to pouch with age, looks stern and amused at the same time.

'Well of course it's true. But I have my fingers in quite enough pies at the moment. I have, for instance, learned to drive a cab. With great difficulty I might say, but all for a good cause. You are still willing I take it? You'll certainly never be forgiven if you aren't.'

'Yes, I gave my word,' says Mrs Audley Jones, shutting the papers into her bag.

32

*

Sunlight has woken Clara and Michael, pricking through the weave of the curtain, white winter sunshine coming from just above the eyes, half pretty, half painful if you look up too soon. Washing her face in cold water, Clara hears the drag and patter of different feet to and from the closet at the end of the passage, and laughs. They were the first this morning. She feels a stretch coming in her body like a slow smile, and pushes the sashes up. The yard looks bare and strange with the lines empty – she does it out of respect for Michael's Sunday – it looks like someone else's yard.

I'm somewhere else, I'm not really here, she catches herself thinking. What do I mean, I'm not really here? The thought tickles pleasantly.

'You look very handsome today,' says Michael as he finishes cutting his nails over the paper on his lap, and adds, 'I'll be going to Mass.' Clara nods. I'm not really here. What sins does he commit anyway, that he should spend his day off in a church?

'Will you come too?' he asks wistfully, not thinking today of hell, nor of the question Father O'Malley will ask, its answer requiring confession, but simply of the pleasure of her company.

'Yes,' Clara says, 'I will today.'

Clara is walking with her husband to the church, both his faded hair and hers, still dark, slick from the comb, their hands smelling of soap and all the streets come up clean in the sun. Not really there, she sees them both, the God-fearing carpenter's man with his tired face and shiny jacket walking to mass with the unbelieving wife who's come between him and peace of mind. She's stifled his child and never asked for absolution, she's disgraced him in parish after parish, yet he walks with her, arm in arm, glad she's come. Unknown to him, she's left her bastard to take its chance on the back steps of the rich, and now, secretly, she will have his second child cut out of her before it has the lungs to breathe with. They are like two hollow dolls and only she knows of the other dolls inside. They are like two broad-shouldered figures from the past, their details picked out in sunlight and memory.

Something has set her free. One of her thoughts-not-in-words tells her that it's because of what she's decided that she's free. It's a feeling of escape as if she's just caught herself from falling, the same rushing release that flooded through her as she turned away from that silent cot all those years ago.

The church is so dark that she can see only the windows, huge expanses of multi-coloured light delicately veined with black. The place is full of quiet endless echoes. She holds on to Michael until the last possible moment, he, not having gazed at the windows can still see in the dark, and guides her to an empty pew, then crosses the aisle to sit among the men. Smells like autumn in here, she thinks, damp and bitter and sad. Michael is kneeling, head bowed, eyes dropped shut final as blinds. He won't look at her now she's here. She wants, impossibly, to hold his arm as slowly in the shuffling silence she returns from not-here to find she is pressed hard, kneeling on wood, while the church groans with miserable, endless chanting and organ chords, each note as long as it possibly could be, like they're trying to make you weep. Each sound takes hold of her and pulls and wrings inside. She feels herself setting solid inside her Sunday best dress and new coat from Mrs Audley Jones: Clara Riley with her feet growing cold holding the little black book shut when everyone else's is open, following the standing and kneeling like a bad dancer in the chorus line. Church is like cleaning floors, she thinks, and her knuckles crack loudly as she pulls herself up again using the book ledge. All around her they are praying for forgiveness, in almost-unison, begging to be cleansed, steady rhythms of chant thudding and falling at the end of each breath. Yes, it's like rinsing in the sink, the sound of it, oh Lord, they're all washing their dirty souls in the huge stone walled sink of the church. She keeps her eyes open throughout the prayer, watching the swaying row of bowed heads in front of her and comparing the set of individual pairs of shoulders. She watches Michael's profile. His face seems sealed up like a stranger's, without the glimpse of his half-blue eyes. His hands rest useless on his knees like sleeping kittens: he's not there, she realises. Just as she was somewhere else walking along in the sunshine this morning, so now he's somewhere else even farther away, not himself. That's the real reason, she thinks, glad to understand.

The pattern in the nearest window is Mary dressed in a thousand fragments of blue, and an angel in gold and red. Pie-faced Mary she thinks, with amusement and a touch of jealousy: better than sneaking the bundle up a stranger's drive at dusk, to call your bastard the Son of God and turn it all to the good . . . And now they're queuing up for communion, Michael glancing at her from the corner of his eye. She looks away. There's something in her insides that writhes at the thought. It's Sunday, the day of ease, the church windows may filter their meagre allowance of light into a coloured gloom, but outside she knows is bright and clear. The bone-dry biscuit, the blood-bitter wine. No.

Instead, she sits on the new-painted wrought iron seat in the churchyard, her swollen hands concealed in black gloves. In Mrs Audley Jones's coat she might almost be taken for a lady. She smiles experimentally, a small, tight smile with the lips only. Michael, shamed, will say that she has been taken giddy. He does not like the new coat because it's too grand and because it's unearned. A debt imposed rather than a gift. The thick coat seems to surround her without touching her. Inside, she's invisible, sitting in the sun thinking what-if thoughts. What-if it was Sunday and we lived in a house like the Rosenburys'? We'd go back to luncheon, all served on hot plates with lots of silver knives. Soup and fish and meat all one after the other, and afterwards, instead of cleaning plates, I'd go upstairs and change into a different dress; spend the afternoon paying calls to my friends . . . Clara knows she is lonely. Every now and then they have to move, in case of talk, Michael says, or because of silence, sometimes worse. It had been in the papers after all. The places had become smaller and smaller, and now this one was the worst. In each

35

new street you waited until things stopped seeming strange, until you were meeting eyes and noticing differences in regular comings and goings. Then you were there, and hopefully found someone you could rely on once in a while. But then you'd be away again. Best keep ourselves to ourselves, he said. Home now is off the street, only the yard full of her own washing to see and steps in the passage she could fit faces to, but they hadn't settled, not in over a year. Perhaps something shows in my eyes. More likely his. Gossips. Gossips would say she'd got above herself, refusing communion to sit in the sun in her fancy coat, full of empty-headed thoughts. That O'Malley stares at me when he talks of sin. Thinking what-if thoughts always brings me back to now, but why you think of them of course is to get away from what is now.

Slowly, figures emerge from the church, blinking in the sun. Michael is one of the last and walks up to her adjusting his hat, his expression quite calm, but tinted with a confused mixture of affection, reproach and resignation. It's a weak face, she thinks suddenly, shocked at herself, weak.

They walk arm in arm, as Clara remembers they did when courting. They met at the Free Evening Institute and each night he walked her to the end of her street. She would allow him no further, but let the darkness swallow and conceal the dilapidation of the area. Months passed and Clara's handwriting grew smaller and decked with little flourishes; the columns of her long division marched down the slate astounding her with their correctness, and Mr Riley, not stopping, not even slowing down as they walked, explained that he worried about her in the night. What would become of her, a woman of irregular and menial employment? He often wondered that. He confessed he had made a journey in the daytime to see where she lived. Without meaning to give offence, it was a bad place. He knew, of course, that she was a good woman, and he had seen her at the institute trying to rise above her circumstances by education. Clara remembers that this phrase took her fancy and she interrupted him, 'Yes, Mr Riley, I suppose I would like to rise above my circumstances.'

They came then to the end of her street and stopped at the corner.

Some poor women were driven to vice, he said. He would like to offer his help and protection, such as it was. Would she marry him? It would be an honour. They would have companionship in the evenings too: the evenings are long and lonely for a man who has little taste for drink, and two people burn the same amount of gas. 'I've no family,' he said, 'but for the church.' That was all that was said at the time of religion. He spoke with all his aitches in; Clara was touched. She caught her breath and kept her silence about the baby born and gone, swaddled in darkness on the edge of the warmth and light of someone else's life, about the money she'd taken from the man. She'd promised herself in the intake of a breath it would be a clean new page. After this, never another lying silence, never another blot or correction. She took her chance gratefully. She didn't ask for time to consider.

'Yes, Mr Riley,' she said, 'I will, if you're sure.'

The ring's a small lump beneath her glove. Washing's made it thin, but her fingers are too swollen to remove it. She'd had to be converted of course, more of a trouble than she thought it would be, and here they were now coming away from the church and to this day she likes it no better.

'Shall we go to the park?' she says. 'Do you remember the Evening Institute? That time when Mrs Enfield brought fancy cakes and played the piano? Do you remember that room with the fire?'

'I remember it.' He pauses. 'What came of it though, all that studying? Supposed to make you something better, but look at me, I've no need really for such things.'

Clara is silent. She now has a lady's coat and a lady's handwriting, that's what comes of it. She remembers something about geometry, the sound of the words for things, but she's forgotten what they refer to: hypotenuse, equilateral. During the war they'd bought newspapers and read them aloud after tea, but hardly ever now.

'This work I'm doing for Mr Holden,' Michael says as they

turn into Hyde Park, 'is very good class. He's using walnut and mahogany, even where it won't be seen. Blunts a plane in half the time of deal. And twice the weight. You'll have seen it in Penley Square, walnut: it's got the grain all swirled together, a pattern like oil and water mixed.' Clara sees it perfectly, the oil and the water, then the wood on Mrs Audley Jones's dressing table reflected in the three mirrors you can tilt to see your back and sides. She can also see their own small mirror, propped on the mantelpiece, moved each morning to the sink for Michael's shaving. Their mirror reflects a much smaller piece of the world. Body and soul, she hungers for walnut and mahogany, for huge, glittering reflections, the smells of polish and out-of-season flowers.

They're approaching Speakers' Corner and Clara resists the pull of Michael's arm steering her away.

'Let's listen a minute,' she says. 'Let's see what they're saying.' They move towards the tangle of people in their Sunday hats and the sound of raised voices above the grumbling of the crowd. Before she's distracted Clara asks Michael, 'What did you confess?' She often wonders.

'Yes,' he replies, only hearing her last word and seeing the question in her face.

'I've got scars from the great war – ' a man shouts.

'Show 'em then, go on,' comes from the crowd.

'*What?*' Clara looks Michael full in the face.

He lowers his eyes, 'Sins of thought,' he mutters.

'The labouring classes have no alternative – ' Michael is continuing his list of sins, but Clara can no longer hear him.

'Science has disposed of the existence of God,' a thin elderly voice enunciates.

'God created science,' thunders another, solid and deep.

'If only the humble working man were to wake and realise what power lies in his weary hands, what worlds he could build, instead of building brick by brick his own grave, hush, no, I tell you, the means whereby – '

All around her voices: blasphemies, insults, arguments, everyone saying anything they want to, loud and ten times over. Clara feels it spinning her like a roundabout, her feet flying off the ground, her tongue loosened in sympathy. Relentlessly she turns back to Michael and asks, 'D'you ever confess about me then?' Her voice is harsh, almost contemptuous. The court knew, Michael knew, Mrs Audley Jones knew, the neighbours got to know. Why confess something not even secret?

'No,' he says, 'I can't confess another's sins, but only my part in them and my weakness in not bringing you to your own confession. Your sin is one of those that cries to heaven for vengeance. God's laws are different from men's.' Michael's face is crumpled, memory running across it like a gale. Clara can't bear his answer or his misery. She spins away, but 'Oh God,' she thinks, 'he's been good to me, poor soul.' She whirls away but her hand is still gripping his arm so she pulls him with her and he stumbles.

'Oh, I'm sorry,' she says, and the word seems so useless, a scrap of scrim to stem a flooding tide of blood; she can't abide his pity nor his pitiful half-forgiveness; she can't abide his misery, his confessions. She can't bear hurting him further, she can't bear to raise children, nor even the weight of her own desires. If she were to stand on a box in the park, a hateful sound would come out, but no proper words. She pulls Michael to where a woman, dressed severely in black silk, stands on a pallet in the midst of the crowd. The woman clutches a white handkerchief which she folds and unfolds as she speaks.

'Drudgery, drudgery,' she repeats in a voice refined in tone, but slightly hoarse, 'drudgery and idleness are the Scylla and Charybdis between whose jaws woman flounders, inevitably sucked by virtue of birth or marriage to one or the other. Why? The answer is in the laws of the land which deprive her of independence and influence alike, and hamper the development of her physical strength and intellectual capacities alike – '

Someone laughs loudly, 'Intellectual capacities,' he repeats scornfully, 'and pray where do those reside in the female anatomy?'

The woman's words are muddled by the laughter of the crowd until they emerge again, 'The right of a married woman to earn her own living, own her own property, have control of her children, to refuse conjugal access – '

There is jeering, and shouts of 'Disgraceful, disgraceful.' The crowd stiffens and flexes like a muscle preparing itself for violent effort; laughter has given way to grunts and snarls and Michael is pulling Clara's arm. Frightened, she follows. Looking back, as they ease their way through the crowd that presses in the opposite direction, she sees Mrs Audley Jones take to the platform as the first speaker retires. Clara doesn't want to be seen. She ducks her head and pushes on, panic rising in her throat.

'Six or seven children bind a woman more surely than prison bars. Even a single child can be the final burden that breaks her spirit. Motherhood may be a joy, but sometimes it is a burden . . . ' Mrs Audley Jones is speaking now. The other speakers have been deserted, stand forlorn as statues, their words falling only on the churned ground. 'Sin, sin' Clara hears as they pass the last, hurrying home.

Mrs Audley Jones, though thinking of Clara as she spoke, did not see her. Mechanically she cleans the remains of rotten fruit from the lapel of her coat. Some of the insults hurled at her still ring in her ears, 'Barren and bitter, that's what she is.' 'Take that banner off, you're no woman.' She stands behind the pallet now, and someone else is calming the crowd she has enraged. Words are worse than useless, she thinks, or I am.

'You'll have to be more careful in the sentiments you express, Christine,' says the tall slender woman standing beside her, 'if you don't wish to provoke a riot. The working classes are not yet ready for the regulation of fertility, I'm afraid.'

'It was people of my own class who jeered the loudest,' says Mrs Audrey Jones, 'and I believe there are many women who are desperate, rather than merely ready.'

'There are other places to express such opinions. We have a

cause here that must not be endangered. Enfranchisement first, all else after, that is what I say – ' Faint applause signals the end of the last speech, police appear on the edges of the crowd, and the two women move quickly to unhitch the large banner they have been standing by. They shake and fold the banner between them, moving together and apart. Her companion takes the thick bundle and makes the last fold over her arm.

Clara's belly feels tight. We've eaten well, she thinks, feeling with her tongue the soft strands of meat stuck between her teeth and savouring them again in memory. Then she remembers the other reason for that bloating of her flesh and the feeling of contentment flickers, threatens to disappear. She fights for it.

'I've decided,' she mutters, 'properly.'

The food and the humid warmth of their room, coming after church and the long walk to the park, have made her muscles soft: it's as if only her clothes keep her in shape. From the shifting red darkness behind her eyes she hears Michael filing his saw, a sound that seems to come from another world, receding, nowhere. She opens her eyes, sees the room, her husband standing by the window to get the last of the daylight, her sewing on the table. But she's forgetting to struggle against sleep, enjoying capitulation.

She watches a child sleep. Its face is purplish, eyes calmly shut, mouth unmoving. It's daytime and the child lies on the far corner of the bed, away from the light. She does not recognise the child. Its lips are curved up in steady pleasure, serene. Clara's eyes feel as if she has been weeping for days. Her breasts hurt. Michael leans over the bed and touches the tiny bunched hands as if to show her how. 'Ssh,' he says, 'Father O'Malley will be coming soon.' She turns away, picks up the iron and holds it for a few seconds, feeling its weight that erases wrinkles, flattens folds. The weight grows enormous in her hand. She can hear church bells from several directions at once, unsynchronised, up and down, up and down. She's

41

frightened. What is it like to kill? What passions seethe and soar, evaporate the flesh and intoxicate the mind? Or will it be dumb and blank? Clara should know, she's done it in her waking life, yet dreaming, there's nothing but the weight in her hand and an overpowering will for there to be nothing she cannot bear –

The noise of filing stops, and Clara, interrupted by the silence, hides behind closed eyes, her heart thumping steadily, she can feel it where her arms touch the table. Her head is hanging down loose from her shoulders. She hears the scrape of Michael's chair on the tiles, crack of flexed finger joints, a few steps, and, almost making her jump, the dry touch of his lips on the back of her neck where short, soft baby hairs stray loose. The door closes softly.

Clara begins to cry silently, not because of the dream, but because of the soft touch on her neck, the hardness of the table she leans over. There have been few loved ones in Clara's life and death or distance have so often taken them from her; she has never felt jealous or possessive of people. But, for as long as she can remember, she has envied: envied strangers, coveted their houses, clothes and shrub-filled gardens; she has wished for other people's faces, bodies, lives: hankered after something larger than all of these that she can't put a name to; it's more even than money, but a lot to do with it – it's a kind of oblivious easiness that carries with it the possibility of adventure, streaks of daring like comets in the sky.

Clara clings fiercely to such feeble imitations of these wants as she's achieved. When she has to choose, she estimates which alternative will bring her most comfort, however little time it lasts. She's aching hungry for comfort. There's never enough. Now, the pleasures in her life are dreamless sleep in clean sheets, wearing Mrs Audley Jones's coat and eating her crustless sandwiches; they are the evenings before it's completely dark, Sundays and certain other days when there's no hurry and she has time to notice things; they are the times she spends imagining herself otherwise situated, more particularly the few spellbound moments when she believes what she has imagined. Clara half despises these pleasures – they are like picture postcards of a place she's never visited, a fraud – but she'll defend them with a passion that might seem disproportionate to those with more appetising choices to make. No one will steal them from her without tasting her venom, sudden and corroding as acid in the face.

The bells are ringing again, the blessed are the meek, the blessed are the poor, the humble, the content, the blessed blooming bells. Clara stuffs her fingers in her ears, stays sitting in the darkened room.

Buttoned in black velvet, only slightly worn, wearing a new hat trimmed with jet beads, Jeanne Biggs has departed to see her sister. Mrs Audley Jones's terms of employment are very generous, and that, coming when she had learned to expect the worst, to scorn men's love and to worry about old age, is one of the reasons Jeanne loves Mrs Audley Jones.

Clara, her face scorched from the fire, nibbles the slightly burnt underside of her piece of fruitcake.

'Would you like more cake, Clara dear?' says Mrs Audley Jones, and Clara controls herself carefully but she's thrown into confusion and humiliation. She swallows the last few crumbs and feels them burning as they pass to her stomach.

'No thank you,' she says, pushing her plate aside and folding her hands on her lap. The burnt cake, she thinks, has probably blackened her tongue. On the carved table with its silver tray and the paraphernalia of tea-making, she's noticed the two other plates, each bearing on its rim a neat finger of cake cut well past the burn.

'It,' begins Mrs Audley Jones, not naming it, 'is against the law, Clara, though it shouldn't be. I felt it only fair to make sure you understood that. Of course, the doctor's discretion is absolutely to be relied on, and I have told him he can expect the same from you. It must be a secret, Clara, do you understand?'

'I'll not be telling,' Clara's voice is hard.

Promise you won't tell, Marcus Rosenbury had said.

'Next Tuesday,' Mrs Audley Jones continues, all of a hurry, excited and relieved, like someone who's concluded a bargain, rushing on fast and strong to sweep aside afterthoughts , 'come here just as usual, but as early as you possibly can. I'll take you to the doctor in a cab. He insists I am to come with you, because ordinarily his lady patients stay overnight nearby, they can make arrangements but – ' Clara squeezes back the laughter that isn't, it settles painfully like wind. Make arrangements! Tuesday is all she need remember. Her eyes follow Mrs Audley Jones's lips and gestures, but the rest of her has burrowed deep inside. ' . . . take you home as late as possible . . . ensure that you have no work to do in the evening . . . '

Mrs Audley Jones smiles brightly. She has just told Clara that she is a brave girl. Now, she takes two large napkins and wraps up the large square cake with its charred bottom and almonds on top in patterns like fancy brickwork.

'Take this home with you, Clara dear,' she says.

Halfway home and carrying three dozen napkins from the Eating House, Clara gives the fruitcake to the girl she once saw collecting leaves, now picking discarded potatoes from the market floor. Afterwards she walks faster, as if she's off-loaded not the cake but the heavy bundle of soiled table linen slung over her shoulder and bouncing erratically on her back as she walks. She turns the interview over in her head, trying to alter it, to rub out the feeling of having been insulted and replace it with gratitude, or at least the comfort of being helped. 'It is against the law, although it shouldn't be' – that was familiar. The barrister Mrs Audley Jones hired for her all those years ago, a comfortable-looking man with brown eyes that swam and melted – he said the law was a crude average reflecting the prejudices of former times, and he would be proud to show it at fault. He'd said they used to hang people for stealing a handful of corn until juries put a stop to it by never finding thieves guilty. 'The law's an ass, and sometimes a sacred cow as well,' he'd said. 'That man, Clara,' said Mrs

Audley Jones, 'is an idealist.' He was dead now. And yes, she could feel grateful to *him*.

Mrs Audley Jones had found and paid Mr Henderson for her, so why doesn't gratitude come?

The law doesn't seem to matter much, and yet Mrs Audley Jones spoke with the flat, slow voice of serious things, each word with space around it so that it didn't get lost. Against – the – law (though it shouldn't be). Discretion. Promise you won't tell. That was what rankled. As if she, Clara, wasn't the one with most to lose!

And yet before, she'd walked out of the door in the morning and confessed to the first constable she met.

'I put a pillow over my baby's head in the night and she's dead.' Why did she tell? She wasn't in her right mind. She looked the constable right in the face and she could see he didn't know what to make of her. She didn't think, she didn't know. This is different, she's not all alone. She'll not be telling anyone.

Thirsty, Clara goes into the Duke of Clarence, orders a beer and sits amidst the noises of eating, drinking and singing. She hasn't been here for years but sits incurious, holding her mug of beer that's dark red like cold tea; she watches the floating bubbles stretch and disappear, doesn't like the taste of it. Against the law, against the law, she repeats to herself in different voices and expressions, trying to see what it really means. Stealing, that's the first thing, she's never done that – no, she has: she used to take home from the houses where she worked slivers of beef and curls of bacon wrapped in her handkerchief, worn nuggets of perfumed soap that should've been boiled down for household use; she's taken rosebuds from gardens at dusk and from big urns of flowers wasting unseen in halls and corridors: – the truth is she's taken things whenever she could. Stealing. It's not so bad, no reason to be punished for taking a few scraps of things no one would miss or need. But against the law. They wouldn't be sorry for you – stealing's the lock up if they catch you.

There's soliciting. I've not done that, not really, and

begging, begging too is against the law: now that should never be punished. She remembers a beggar dragged away from a doorway near the Buildings, a woman in a man's jacket and rags swathed round and round her ankles, struggling so hard it took three to move her, but she made no sound at all. The way the beggar woman was so quiet and so fierce at the same time was what made it stick in your mind.

It seems, she thinks, almost everything the poor might do to get a bit of comfort is against the law. Mind you there are other things, arson and treason and smuggling and deserting the army and assault and –

Murder. The word's been battering steadily away and now it bursts through the brittle wall confining it like some monstrous featherless chick. Murder: they kill you for that, they hang you up and break your neck and people go to see. She's never been, but plenty do. An eye for an eye, Michael said, when the racehorse man was hung, but all along the racehorse man said that it was a mistake, he pushed too hard by accident, and who could ever know the truth. They're offered a priest, nothing's hidden from the eye of God. And hell to come, why bother then? Killing her baby was killing, but not quite murder, not calculated. But Michael had called it murder.

'Something wrong with your beer?' asks the man in the never-come-clean apron, waist to knee a muddle of stains and spills.

'No,' says Clara, taking a few mouthfuls as he watches, 'no, it's good beer', thinking, 'Is it murder, murder that I'm going to do this time? Is it even killing?'

'Only we don't like no loitering here.' It's against the law probably. The man's eyes are bloodshot and shiny. 'Respectable house here,' he continues, taking in the expensive coat, confused by the swollen hands and something, maybe, about her face. He wipes his own wet hands on the dirty apron, perhaps he's made a mistake.

'I beg your pardon,' says Clara, 'I am a respectable woman.'

'I'm sure you are m'dear,' he says over his shoulder, still wiping his hands as he moves back to the bar. There's laughter, brief and spiteful. Clara drinks steadily to fill the silence that seems to be collecting around her. She straightens her back and looks ahead, seeing nothing on purpose. At home, under knives and forks are the newsprint words to prove the barman wrong. 'Respectable, honest, hard-working, not in the least inclined towards drink or vice of any kind,' that's what Mr Henderson had said. And also, he'd said, *Would this woman commit cold-blooded murder of her own issue? Impossible.*

'Come on,' she tells herself, 'drink up, the bloody law will never know in any case. Who's going to tell 'em?' Even the one beer has made her queasy, her sight not quite straight. Or is it the baby? It's all arranged now, secret and sanitary and against the law.

.2.

At midday in a white-painted, brass-plated townhouse tucked behind a tree in the far corner of a park-side square, Clara is wrenched blindfolded into half-birth, struggling in a slurry of wanting to make, but knowing she'll destroy. Flailing down the gulf between dream and experience, wanting, wanting, she gives death to her third birth (and, as she does so, remembers other people's children in white dresses in perambulators in the park, remembers also those final, airless moments of her last child's life). Who's brave enough for the truth and who's ever sure? The disappointment of pushing always against the grain of a life that might be, pushing for and against her body and soul, confused: disappointment – the word is poor and small to what she sees in her damned mind's eye, but it sees, it sees and after it's seen, Clara lives in drizzling shadows, Clara clutches, clutches and strangles in the shadows of if only, the power of her wanting. What is it? What are they doing to me? Biting her lips to keep the noises in, don't make a sound, don't tell. If wanting otherwise could sear through reality, tear it aside like a rotten curtain, then Clara would be so very different, but reality's thick as fog and sharp as a knife and what little she can do is only to cut out the disappointment in her own flesh. Clara knows what is being done in the dark, there's no anaesthetic and the pain's in layers like hot rock, and she can't do it for herself, even this.

Clara almost thinks she cannot bear it any more and a hand is pressed tight over her mouth, she's blindfolded, her nose not big enough to breathe through; but she keeps thinking 'I wanted this, I wanted this' in time to the pain, otherwise it would be the death of her, and so she remains for the whole time conscious, rigid in stifling dark, mind's eye and hearing her only senses.

'Keep your hand over her mouth.'

'I'm not accustomed to take risks for women of this kind.'

'The devils.'

'Water, quickly.'

'Do you hear me? I tell you, don't make a sound.'

Clara lets the air out between her teeth, slowly. The bandage around her eyes is drenched. Something has been stuffed into her mouth. She tries to pull it out, it's her tongue.

Later, there's water smelling of carbolic, stinging and sputtering inside like spit on a heated iron. Another smell, of lavender water dashed on her forehead by Mrs Audley Jones, then the searing stench of salts of ammonia; she opens her eyes and sees a face puckered with anxiety.

'Clara, Clara.'

I'm alive, thinks Clara.

'That's better – ' says Mrs Audley Jones, 'the doctor says it was hard, so you've been very brave.'

The dabbing on her forehead enervates Clara but she's too weak to complain. She feels as if everything, even the worst of her memories, has been bleached away in the pain and ironed flat in the sleep after; it's as if the ordeal was some strange kind of sacrament and now she lies pure and purged. The scars she feels already stitching themselves together inside her are thicker and more durable than the softness that was there before and she feels in her flesh that this will never happen again, none of it. She feels thankful to Mrs Audley Jones for the first time.

'I'm glad it's done,' she says, and Mrs Audley Jones weeps a little into the scent-drenched handkerchief, apologises; advises on hygiene and the staunching of blood, wound-blood not monthly-blood it is, hotter and faster, warmly seeping on to the thick pad of folded linen between her legs. Mrs Audley Jones leaves the room and returns with a cup of barley broth.

Outside it is still light and there's an hour until the cab will come.

'Think, Clara,' says Mrs Audley Jones gently, 'what it would be to live in a world where this sort of thing never had to happen . . . ' Clara recognises Mrs Audley Jones as a thinker of what-if thoughts, albeit of a thin and fleshless kind, and smiles.

Encouraged, Mrs Audley Jones continues, 'Clara, I begin to think that these oppressions thrust upon women seemingly by nature are no less than a conspiracy perpetuated by men against women. I have fought against accepting some of the more radical opinions of my militant sisters but in the end it must be admitted the evidence is with them, and it is not a matter of mere opinion. My second marriage has perhaps forced such thoughts upon me. I thought it better to be a wife in my husband's house than a daughter in my father's. It has been so, but only in that I have more privacy. A few years later my choices would have been quite different. Clara, we promise to serve and obey: why should a person serve and obey what goes against her own best interests, her conscience, her health? Imagine a life free from coercion . . . If, for example, your husband was enlightened enough not to deny you the protection of preventative measures, if such measures were readily available, if you had never needed to marry – '

'I don't really mind – relations,' says Clara. 'It's not much.'

'But the consequences, Clara, for a service often offered purely for the husband's benefit; if you think of the consequences to yourself, then you must mind, surely?' Mrs Audley Jones is pleading, exasperated. 'What you have suffered today . . . and before . . . is a consequence, don't you see, Clara?'

'Yes,' says Clara, feeling, however, that there are other consequences and complications to contend with.

Mrs Audley Jones has begun again, speaking now of financial

independence for women. 'So you wouldn't need, Clara, to feel obliged. Clara, I'm not tiring you am I?' Her eyes are big rounds as if the lids have shrunk away; the pupils, big with excitement, are not seeing the room.

'No,' says Clara, but Mrs Audley Jones's words do not inspire her. They mingle with the pain that crouches in her womb, forbidding even the smallest movement. None of the stuff of Mrs Audley Jones's dreams is going to happen to her – pie in the sky she thinks, fancy dreams like fancy cakes: she's got the time to have them.

'The lot of all women, however situated, is in certain respects similar. We are a class, like Labour. I dream of a women's party in Parliament – ' She takes Clara's hand in hers. Clara begins to cry, easy coming tears like night-time rain.

Clara sits quietly watching London through the small mud-spattered window. The journey home is through the very heart of the city where the gents, stiff and black, march clockwork in and out of offices and marble-faced banks. Mrs Audley Jones is shivering, but there is a thick plaid rug on Clara's knees. In the West End Clara watches young girls with their aunts and mothers dressed in pale shades of lavender, dove and fawn with little umbrellas to match. She looks at them without, for once, riffling bitterly through her sparse memories for comparisons with her own girlhood, appearance, suitors, possibilities, happiness or lack of it, but instead she stares out at the scurrying tea-time world with the detachment of one so far removed from it as to feel barely human. What she has done seems to have set her apart even from what she herself used to be.

'You shouldn't do any work,' repeats the woman by her side anxiously.

'The soup's already made,' says Clara.

'Here are your wages – '

'I didn't collect the washing.'

'Never mind, Clara, take it just the same.'

Clara takes the envelope, weighing the feel of it in her hand: there's more than her due in there. She holds it loosely in her lap, indifferent.

Clara's blood seeps gently as she walks slowly from table to sink to yard, and at first she feels triumphant as she did when she first bled as a girl, though her pride, like the blood itself, is thinner and more brilliant now. Sometimes for minutes on end there is a pain that makes her dizzy, and then nothing; nonetheless she's beginning to be happy. She doesn't doubt the blood will dry up and the invisible inside damage mend itself. Termination has worked its secret unguessed. There was three weeks' money in the envelope from Mrs Audley Jones, so she has bought a hat and satin ribbons to trim it with, and a bar of lavender soap that's hidden in an empty paste jar beneath the sink; she catches the smell of it every time she bends to set a bowl on the floor.

'Second time this week,' says the eel woman to Clara as she counts out her change. 'Come into a little something, have you? You can taste the sea in my eels, the sea itself.'

'You can that,' replies Clara, smiling, the inside of her mouth straining to imagine what sea might taste like. The eel-seller folds Clara's fingers over her change, chuckling quietly; her hands are small and grimed with money-dirt, bluish-black from copper and bronze. Clara's hands are always clean; countless daily immersions seek out even dirt buried in creases, her hands are as clean as the lace-trimmed sheets she returns weekly to Mrs Audley Jones, but crumpled. 'Opposites', Clara thinks, but feels a kinship with the eel woman, a little pocket of warmth trapped between their work-spoiled fingers.

They have eels twice a week for a month. Michael's seen the sea but never had the taste of it. They take to going for a walk together before their tea if the weather's fine, Clara moving with caution, stiff at the waist and almost ladylike. Her face is pale and sick-looking but she's cheerful.

'I see them in the morning, going to the factory,' she says to Michael as they watch the lipsticked girls walking out in the dusk. 'I'm glad I've never been forced to factory work, and now I'm old enough that they wouldn't have me.'

'No satisfaction in that kind of work,' he replies. 'Machines'll have your arm off if you don't look out.'

He returns late from work, coughing from the dust and talkative only as long as hunger nags him. 'The years I've been with the trade,' he says, 'and it's still as hard as ever it was to get work and keep it, and each day long and hard as well.' He shrugs. 'My cross,' he says.

Clara knows he has, at times, seen her in the same way. She gets up, leaving her food unfinished, walks around the table and stands behind him, and holding his shoulders rests her head briefly in the hollow where his neck joins his body. The words that first come to mind are 'Michael, I do hope you have really forgiven me the past' – but to speak them she would have to risk her happiness and destroy their calm with backwards looking. 'Who knows,' she says instead, 'what the future will bring.' Of that also she is reluctant to think, though less so and there's a softness in her voice which at least leaves room for hope. Michael leans back in his chair; his eyes closing slowly. At least, Clara thinks, the future will bring me no more children; there'll be no more violent ends. The past might leak a little into the present; but at the same time she believes it is safely sealed away, just because she believes it cannot happen again. In her sleep Clara will sometimes be visited by a glimpse of her never-grown offspring, whole and happy and unrecognising. Their smiles bring a sharp little twist of melancholy like the sight of abandoned clothes still stretched to their one-time owner's shape, or lockets with hair in them hanging in pawnshop windows, bits of broken dolls found in parks. But it is a small, swift pain. Clara counts her blessings and squeezes Michael's shoulder before silently re-turning to her meal. Opening his eyes, Michael says, 'Growing old isn't so bad as I thought when I was starting out.' She looks into his face, framed by the doorway behind. So many nights and Sundays it's been there, changing unnoticed like a plant growing in a pot. But now she can see he's indeed older, there's a tiredness which, noticed all of a sudden, seems to fall over his face like a veil of dust that might be wafted away. Michael with slow movements wipes the last traces of his meal from his plate with a piece of bread.

'I'm quite happy,' he says, 'despite what I said, I'm happy of an evening sitting here with you. In spite of – ' He begins, then falters. 'I don't know why,' he mumbles.

Exultant, Clara reaches for his hand across the table. Against all the sayings of the religious, her deceit has brought them peace. A simple little lie it was, only silence when she didn't want to tell. She's won a contentment she knows most people would say she shouldn't rightly have. Her smile is sly and perfect, lips stretched but not parted, like a lady's in a painting, eyes deep-dark with satisfaction, brimming with her secret, and tears of relief.

.3.

Mrs Audley Jones slips and tears her way through the five-o'clock tide of Oxford Street shoppers, keeping close to the polished panes behind which are ranked silks, taffetas, wine, gold and vellum, their rich colours streaking into a bright swathe that seems to become lighter the quicker she moves. Her heart beats even faster than the running warrants. Beneath double layers of clothing her skin flares red and damp.

'This is my hour,' she thinks, 'this is the beginning of the end and we shall win.' Her heartbeat spreads outwards, pounding in lungs, throat, ears, legs, everywhere. 'What if I'm caught? What if I slip and fall?' A fine drizzle refracts the lights and glitter of Christmas decorations. The pavement shines and splutters, the weight of the bag strapped around her waist twists at her back. 'The last resort can't be wrong.'

All thought disappears as she throws the first brick. It seems she hangs in mid-air waiting, but her foot hits the ground and there's nothing but a muted crack as the brick bounces from the window. Oh no! Has anyone seen? And she pushes herself to run yet faster, weaving her way out towards the curb, aware of startled and affronted glances. She must throw high and hard, hard, hard over the hatted heads, quickly too: she hears the first explosive shattering and a tiny scream. Her eyes are shut: pray no one's hurt, no one's coming. Again and again she throws, she can hardly breathe, everywhere the sharp breaking sound, the incoherent smithereens of sound, gasping, shouting: she flings herself through the door of the waiting cab.

They're moving instantly, even though her lungs burn and her legs are dead as metal. She's laughing as Irene struggles to pull the dowdy woollen cloak from her, pulls off the hat, unstraps the brick-bag, unclips the mud-spattered skirt. Neither of them speak. The cab veers round corner after corner and then comes to a stately halt.

'Out with you now,' commands Irene, leaning over to open the door, and Mrs Audley Jones tumbles from the cab dressed in lavender tweed and carrying an umbrella. As the cab departs, she catches a glimpse of Mrs Brett, in cap and jacket, the perfect cabbie, wiping the sweat from her forehead on her sleeve. 'We did it,' she thinks, and it seems at that moment that they could do anything else they chose. She stands for a few seconds to catch her breath, fastens back a strand of damp hair and then walks slowly back in the direction of Oxford Street, her eyes bright and her face flushed.

The *London Record* quotes Miss Amy Leston, a shop assistant who got glass in her face when Mrs Audley Jones threw her bricks: four large gashes and a peppering of tiny splinters that took a surgeon several hours to remove.

'I have never wanted the vote; I have done nothing to deserve this. I would like to see the person that did this to me punished, God help her.' Miss Amy Leston, a young woman whose features and complexion, prior to this vindictive attack, were of great delicacy and beauty, will be scarred for life. She will find it impossible to continue in her present employment.

Mrs Audley Jones has bought another house in Euston, and filled it with homeless and wayward girls.

'Teaches them cooking, cleaning and how to type,' Jeanne tells Clara.

'Young girls can earn more than you and me, typing in offices. And it's light work.'

Because of Mrs Audley Jones's increasing devotion to her cause, and because of her husband's absence, their house at Penley Square is rarely used for any kind of entertaining. It's staffed modestly, considering the Admiral's income, and the servants have little to do. As Jeanne says, there's nothing of a home about it any more.

'She runs in and out to get her letters and a bit of sleep,' Jeanne's voice is half resentful, half admiring, 'looks a shadow of herself. Eaten up, she is, eaten up from inside. "It takes more than words to fight a battle" she said to me the other day.'

'I saw her in the park one Sunday,' says Clara.

'That's not enough now, she says. She's more of a militant every day. Or from what she says she is. But it doesn't come easy to her. Half of them are at each other's throats as to the best way to go about things. It doesn't come easy to her. I found her on the landing one night, her eyes were wide open, but she was fast asleep. I don't know what'll happen when the Admiral gets back. She thinks she can keep it all quiet . . . '

'I've often wondered why she married him,' Clara interrupts.

'Cross my heart, I know as much as you do.' Her eyes are blank: true or not, she'd never tell.

Mrs Audley Jones has arranged for Clara to do the napkins and tablecloths for Onward House, hand-embroidered in green and purple by the once wayward girls: some are neatly stitched, some straggle at the back. The other things they do for themselves. Jeanne and Clara have their tea and sandwiches – cut a little rougher than before – in the kitchen, and Clara's pay, counted out in advance by Mrs Audley Jones, is tucked under the side of her plate for her to take as she leaves.

'You should hear some of the dreams and schemes she comes up with,' Jeanne is saying as Clara picks it up, weighing it. A week ago Michael fell at work and a nail went in his eye. He's flat on his back in darkness: rest is the only possible cure but far from certain.

'I've not the time for her kind of dreams right now,' says Clara.

'How are you managing with him laid up?' says Jeanne. 'You can always come round here, you know, if you're short of something. I know she wouldn't mind.'

'Oh but we're all right really – ' Clara's sudden smile startles Jeanne; it's like another person's face.

The girls in Onward House, many of them in fact women, eat from simple white plates with 'Strive for Freedom' and a small crest printed in green and purple on their rims. Six hours a day the air judders from the battering of twenty typewriters; at eleven and four o'clock hot meals are carried up from the basement by the girls who've cooked them that day. The girls are free to leave at any time, though so far no one has.

Mrs Audley Jones's nights drift from one nightmare to the next, from guilt to dread to an endless torturing mirage of hope. Of course she sent money anonymously to Miss Leston who, in the space of only a week, has received offers of marriage and medical services as well as other gifts, large and small. Only shock tactics will win the vote, lobbying has failed over and over. But splintered glass in the soft face of a woman sho never wanted freedom? When Mrs Audley Jones, the sweat drying deliciously on her face, walked slowly back down Oxford Street and peered casually at her handiwork, roped off and guarded by constables, she was ignorant of Miss Leston's injuries and she had forgotten that she had been afraid. She was proud. But now the enormity of the consequences should she be detected: everything's chaos. Many of her old friends would condemn her action, even without Miss Leston's ruined face. And perhaps even now, her new ones regard it as a failure, just as they regard Onward House as a distraction.

'Keep quiet and don't tell a soul,' said Irene, 'incommunicado.'

As if she would, even though there's part of her that wants to confess, weeping at Miss Leston's knees. What would happen to the girls at Onward House? What would they think? Onward House and all her suffrage work are secret from the Admiral. Soon, when he comes home on leave, all must be packed away like furniture in store. Suppose he finds out all of it, any of it? He's forbidden her. He terrifies her. Defiance and secrecy never mix, but swirl together in agitating kaleidoscopic patterns. Her mind goes white at the thought of all she's done and is doing. Sometimes she doubts its worth. Some say the vote will make no difference. Miss Leston says she's never wanted it.

Four Bricks, wrapped in paper bearing the inscription: 'Votes for Women' were thrown at two shop windows in Oxford Street last Wednesday, damaging windows, merchandise and display cabinets. Miss Amy Leston, a shop assistant at Sedgwick and Pearne's, received severe injuries from splinters of glass impaled in her face. The perpetrator of this senseless and shocking act, which has earned condemnation even from the more rational suffrage organisations, is said to have been a woman of middle age wearing dark clothing of a rather bedraggled and old-fashioned appearance, who ran into a waiting cab which officers of the law have been unable to trace.

This kind of indecent attack on both property and innocent people has occurred some four times in London and twice in Manchester since the beginning of the autumn. It is difficult to imagine what these 'suffragettes' as they are being called hope to achieve by such disgraceful behaviour. This kind of reckless, hysterical lawlessness scarcely recommends the female temperament as one which should share in the stately and deliberate process of elections to Parliament. Should a part in the making of the law be given to those who show themselves unwilling or unable to abide by its canons? The answer is no, never.

Mrs Audley Jones folds the newspaper, offered to her as an example of the fearful nature of the modern world, and places it on the table with an expression of mild and somewhat quizzical interest. She doesn't want to go to prison. She doesn't want to go on hunger strike or be force fed, even though she can see the reasons for it. Still less would she like to go as a failure who succeeded only in hurting another woman. She can't endanger Onward House. In Onward

House, it's absolutely clear to her that what she does is of value. She will not throw another brick, even though Irene says that Miss Leston will probably be happy in the end, married and better off than before.

'Not one of our girls has shown the slightest desire to return to the kind of life she was forced to lead before,' she says to the Bishop, a white-faced man slumped in his chair as awkward and graceless as a fish on a marble slab, growing stale and glazed by the minute. She wants money for Onward House.

'Excellent work, excellent.' His teacup rocks dangerously as he clears his throat.

'Some more tea?' Mrs Audley Jones smiles unblinkingly, because if she closes her eyes she will be back on Oxford Street, her blood up, her breath scalding, the shiverings of broken glass laughing at her heels . . . but she will not do it again.

Jeanne's information of Clara is grudging and enigmatic. 'Looks like something that laid a golden egg. Or something that stole the cream, I'm sure I don't know which, but she's well enough. Even with her Michael laid up half blind she's well enough . . . '

That at least was something that had not gone wrong. Sitting up late at the little desk she has in Onward House, Mrs Audley Jones resolves to be in next laundry day so as to see Clara, but then remembers that she will not be in London but in Liverpool, giving a lecture to the Townswomen's Guild.

Dear Clara, she writes, her handwriting deliberately bigger and plainer than usual, I remember it is your birthday soon, and of course Christmas is coming. As I am kept so busy here, along with Miss Handley and Miss Wise, I am writing to wish you the very best and to enclose –

She pauses: no appropriate sum leaps to her mind. One week's wages, so much per year of service? Enough to buy a pair of shoes?

– one guinea, for you to spend however you please. I was so sorry to hear of your husband's accident, but I do hope you are

60

in good health yourself, after all your troubles. You must let me or Jeanne know if you have any difficulties. Your friend, Christine Audley Jones.

She leaves the letter with Jeanne, so that Clara can receive it without Michael knowing.

Michael prays for a miracle, lying in darker than darkness on his bed. Oh Lord forgive this sinner and bring back the light. His hands finger the bandage, thick stuff that gives no hint of what's beneath.

'It's not a punishment,' says Clara, 'there's no need to pray for forgiveness. It was a horrible accident. What could anyone want to punish you for? Look, there's extra money from Mrs Audley Jones, and then I've more work from that place of hers – ' as if he was already blind, she folds his hand gently around the coins. 'There's plenty. There's only two of us. Rest . . . '

What if . . . She takes her washing out into the yard to save him from some of the steam. She feeds and comforts him with the unadmiring closeness a woman can have for a man who is not quite able to be one, sweet and strong forever-and -a-day as the love between childhood friends. Clara has fallen in love with the man lying day in day out on the bed, gathering darkness like dust.

Inspector Garvey is taking on new men: a matter of pride with him, since it means he has been deemed successful, efficient and reliable in his judgement. Each new recruit adds to both his responsibilities and his salary. His decisions are instant, but he checks them always with a few questions. 'Beef,' he says to his deputy, 'beef is what to look for. And loyalty. And obedience, honesty. But it all boils down to beef.' He drags his fingers through his beard, which is thickly curled, as yet untouched by the grey which is beginning to grow in his hair, ineradicable as thistles in a field of golden corn. Beef, land, yellow-yolked eggs, good beer, iron and steel and a full day's slog; some people deserve to swing, leave sentiment to foreigners and women, a man's home is his castle; God, King, duty, wife – but Inspector Garvey is reluctant, as usual, to return to his own home and wife.

'You'll do,' he says to the recruit and smiles; a moment of weakness perhaps, or a grimace of fear or impatience as he chases away a momentary vision of the prim, polished, stifling rooms his wife maintains for them: the clusters of lace and pretty plates his shillings pay for, which his sense of the proper applauds but which makes him feel like a horse in a palace. He claps the recruit across the shoulders, enjoying his confusion.

'Part of His Majesty's now, eh? We'll have a jar of ale to celebrate.'

Garvey feels the recruit's muscles alert beneath the starched shirt and too-tight jacket.

In the public house, Garvey gives Edmonds cordial permission to remove his jacket and roll up his shirt-sleeves. 'I'm not your superior until next week,' he tells him, but he feels that he is: cat and mouse, that's what life's about.

'Thank you, sir.'

'This'll be in your line of duty.' Garvey gestures round the bar, then slaps the hefty thigh of his new recruit, name again forgotten, face indistinguishable. Gaslight barely escapes from behind opaque glass shields. There are as many women as men present, all brightly dressed. Growing warm and expansive, Garvey loosens his collar; sometimes a man as big as he feels constrained by chairs and tables and all the other bits and pieces of life. He's hungry, but not for Friday's white fish and lemon pudding waiting for him at home in the quiet, ticking dining room.

'Er – Edmonds, you'll have to come in here regular: to check on the girls. Not the same as it was when the Acts was in force, you could take 'em in – ' His fingers tighten into the loosening flesh of Edmonds' knee. 'On suspicion.' Red, he thinks, fine colour red, red rag to a bull. 'Bit of an eye opener?' he asks the recruit, closing one eye in a wink and opening the other one wide. 'See that one there with the white gloves? Could pull her in right now, the way she's carrying on, the one with cherries in her hat, see?' Edmonds ventures to point out that the one next to her is carrying on even worse. Garvey is pleased. 'Ah, but there you have it, a point of law. Because with that lady in green, it was the gentleman that came up to her. Whereas with Madame Cherry it was distinctly the lady herself who approached the gentleman. See?' He jabs Edmonds in the stomach, then throws himself back in his seat and laughs unaccountably loud. He feels his flesh all loosened and shaking with the laugh, a real pleasure it is to laugh so, heaving and sweating with good humour. 'A Point of Law,' he repeats, to reprovoke his own mirth. 'Mind you, you can always stretch a point.' Edmonds is still smiling timidly, his eyes fixed on the woman in green satin. Together they take long pulls on their beer. 'Mind you,' says Garvey, not laughing now but suddenly confidential, father to son, 'what you might do, in order to – confirm your – suspicions – is to stand close to the lady in green – not to speak or look, mind you, just stand close and idle. And then if she were to approach you – solicit – '

'Would that be in the way of my duty, sir?'

'It would,' Garvey says slowly, smiling, 'be neither here nor there, soliciting is the offence.' There is a moment's hesitation, Edmonds wondering whether his moral mettle is being tested. 'Nothing simpler,' continues Garvey, an edge to his voice like a taint on butter. 'You establish whether or not the woman is what's called a "lady of the night" – a whore. You are the only witness, an officer of the law, it could be said you were doing your duty.' Garvey's laughter breaks out again, shaking his belly. The recruit laughs too. 'Besides, you're still a mister until Monday next.'

Garvey leans at the bar drinking, while Edmonds stands by one of the dark red marbled columns. Edmonds, thinks Garvey, has a lot to learn, but he'll definitely do. He watches the woman in green turn and mouth a few indistinguishable words to Edmonds, no longer slouching but standing bolt upright as if he was talking to blue blood. Edmonds' eyes, bright with panic, flicker in Garvey's direction. Garvey carries

63

the glasses of brandy he's just paid for over to the column, and gives them one each. The woman in green puts her hand on Edmonds' arm and turns towards him, looking over her shoulder. She says sarcastically, 'Is that gentleman coming with us?'

Garvey hates them, their coarse laughter and whiplike tongues, their bright eyes looking you up and down with no respect, a kind of contemptuousness they have. They smell of paint and pox, he thinks to himself, paint and pox. Brandy, anger, disgust and jealousy run confused in his veins as he follows Edmonds and the woman in green across the back courtyard and up carpetless stairs, keeping close enough to hear the woman's scalding laughter and fragments of Edmonds' hesitant pleasantries. The two stop for a moment, and Garvey, a little breathless, comes to a halt on the landing below. He can see the woman from the waist down, her full satiny green skirt, black patent shoes, white stockinged ankles. That green is the colour of vice, he thinks, the very colour and measure of it.

'Well, I never,' she's saying, 'I shall take it as an honour. A man needs a bit of know-how if he's to be wed.' She moves on, leading Edmonds, now silent, to the uppermost of the rooms. She leaves the key in the lock on the inside, but Garvey runs his hand up the door until he finds the place where the old lock used to be, a large splintered hole where the door was broken in. He watches Edmonds hand over some coins, he watches Edmonds' back as he clutches the green silk to him, watches the woman guide Edmonds through the motions of the brief act that nightly draws crowds to this particular public house. Edmonds' bottom soon thrashes energetically and confidently into the centre of a tousled heap of green satin and white petticoat. He shouts like a man wounded in battle, and Garvey feels his own erection dissolve into wetness, then takes the steps down quickly but a little unsteadily, so as to wait for Edmonds in the bar, now thick with people and nowhere to sit.

Edmonds leaves the woman in green, thinking of his fiancée, whom he considers an altogether different kind of girl. He is ashamed he cried out, feeling it to have been unmanly, and ashamed that he told her of his innocence. Another time, he thinks, but no, there won't be another time. He finds it difficult to meet Garvey's eyes. 'Time to go home,' Garvey comments blearily. 'Seven o'clock sharp on Monday': just the tone of his voice is enough –

'Yes, sir,' says Edmonds, the night's experiences helter-skeltering into a small dark recess at the back of his mind.

'I don't stand sloppiness of dress, timekeeping or hand-writing,' adds Garvey, half snarling. To both of them disci-pline is as calming as the cold outside air through which they walk, straight-backed, apart, but their feet in step, the click of their shoe-segs on the pavement like the winding of a winch.

Lizzie, the woman in green, is in low spirits despite the good money she's earned. She guesses Edmonds will be back at the 'Albert', if not to her. Virgin men over a certain age always go to whores, she thinks, and whilst that's good for business, and she's used to the degradation of what she once did for love alone, she sometimes finds overwhelmingly depressing the evidence that such degradation is, among men, almost universal.

'It's a shame, a crying shame,' she mutters to Cherry as they walk home together in the dawn. 'In one way he was a nice young man, in another he wasn't. Of course, to him I'm just a filthy whore.'

'Your heart's too big for a person of your means'. Cherry is uncomfortable with melancholy. 'Look, the sun's going to shine. I wish I was awake to see it once in a while.'

'Need different clothes for the day, the light's so searching.' They have coffee and eggs in the first place they come to. Lizzie starts again. 'I was quite touched when he told me. Felt sorry I'd taken the money, wished – '

Cherry begins laughing uncontrollably, has to put down her knife and fork and clutch the edge of the table, but Lizzie continues, 'But by the end, of course, he'd changed, same as any of them he was.'

'Oh, Liz, what have you been drinking to make you so maudlin?'

65

Lizzie ignores the question. 'I get so tired,' she says, 'I think I've got something again, as well, I shouldn't work for a while, but – '

'Money, money,' Cherry intones, the little word that says it all and spoils the sunshine. Lizzie is openly weeping by the time they leave the Corner House, and Cherry takes her arm. 'You're not well, sweetie. You'll be yourself tomorrow, after a bit of shut-eye, now, won't you?'

Mr William Elverton leaves his chambers early, not tired but bored, his nerves uneasy. In the entrance hall he meets Inspector Garvey, to whom he must force himself to be civil, since it is to Garvey that he owes his regular employment as a prosecution barrister and his considerable reputation as a young man of talent and prospects. Elverton needs his work, or rather the social rewards it brings, much as other men of his class need their wives, horses, collections and houses. Tonight he is to attend a dinner given to mark the return of Admiral Audley Jones: he will be the youngest man there and also, he is determined, the most brilliant in serious conversation. His brushed and pressed clothes will cling to his spare frame, a visible aura of *savoire faire*; his long-boned hands will cut his meat as efficiently as his mind slices and sorts words and arguments. He wants his hosts and their guests to be a little in awe of him, slightly afraid but not enough to dislike him. He will drink, but only moderately. Elverton has a gift for imagining himself in most situations before they happen, and then of making his imagining real.

He decides to take Garvey to his club rather than climb back up the dark polish-smelling staircase, its handrail now dull after a day's use. They walk, although long walks make Garvey breathless.

'I'm afraid I am somewhat pressed for time, Inspector Garvey,' Elverton says, as they arrive, 'but may I offer you some refreshment?'

Garvey refuses, but Elverton senses this is only because he is rather inhibited by the luxury of his surroundings. He orders a glass of sherry and a biscuit for himself, watching Garvey closely, as a scientist might observe the behaviour of a particular animal under certain conditions.

'As a matter of fact,' Garvey says after a few moments of silence, 'I think a glass might set me up after all, it's been a long day,' and Elverton feels he has the measure of the man. There's skill, he thinks, not only in the use of words but also in the tactics of silence. He nods and orders another sherry. He waits for Garvey to speak.

'There's a case – strictly between you and I', Garvey speaks in a low voice, pausing exaggeratedly to finish swallowing his biscuit, which, despite elaborate precautions showers his chest with crumbs, 'a case where we'll be treading on thinnish ice, if you know what I mean . . . ' A pause. 'If you're interested, I could mention a few things beforehand . . . '

'What kind of affair is it?' asks Elverton. Garvey's mannered attempts at being a gentleman of the world irritate him by their ineptness.

'It's a question of a young woman who killed her husband. Everything's there; rat poison bought at a certain shop, times of going here and there, meals unshared . . . there's been hundreds of cases like it. But none of it's completely watertight. Now you know how these things can go; pretty little woman stands up in the dock and sheds a few crocodile tears – '

'Difficult to convince a jury of the guilt of a woman who looks like their favourite daughter,' says Elverton, 'but not, of course, impossible.'

'What's missing, and what we need, is motive. The husband apparently was of regular habits, given to occasional drinking, but always respectful to his wife. A religious man, who allowed his wife the purse strings to such an extent she really had nothing to gain by his death. A faithful husband. No motive, and yet she poisoned him, no doubt of it. If we had a motive, it would all fall together like a jigsaw.'

'I see,' says Elverton, 'and what class of person is the woman?'

'She's a lady. It'll be an important affair.'

'All women carry within them things not apparent on the surface. Malice. Deception. Follies and dreams.'

Elverton can't refuse the chance to earn fear or respect, or both, from those he dines with. Also he dislikes women intensely; they lie and conceal and they mostly do it badly, and a woman that lies well, he believes, will always admit to it in the end out of boastfulness or guilt. One way or another they're sloppy creatures with no pride and too much influence. He also believes that women harbour grudges against men. His own mother had said when he told her of his intention to read Law: 'Were the world not organised so as to prevent me, that is the sort of profession that I would have chosen.' His mother was a sickly woman who spent much of her time reading or crying. 'That is an absurdity,' he had answered. 'Had I the choice,' she replied, her mild face transformed suddenly by an expression of utter bitterness, 'I should have preferred a daughter. Young men are insufferably arrogant. I hope you prove yourself worthy of your opportunities.' He hated her for that, but her words have haunted him. Every day since he has proved his worth, stated and restated his superiority and made sure of the good opinion of everyone who matters. He will never have hers. Every woman he meets reminds him of her.

'I think I may be of some use,' he says, his face giving the impression of slight abstraction, as if trying to recall an entry in his diary. 'We shall discuss it later, I am already late.' He leaves Garvey struggling into his too-tight coat with the assistance of a footman, and goes home to dress.

Jeanne Biggs, ostensibly arranging flowers, lingers by Mrs Audley Jones's unspoken invitation in the dressing room. She fidgets with the freesias and mimosa, glancing often at the winged mirror's splintered image of Mrs Audley Jones, whose hands hang earrings and stab brooches on her dress as an overworked nanny might adjust the hat of a child not to be trusted to do it for herself. Jeanne Biggs wants to ask a question, but something she calls 'respect' inhibits her.

'The worst possible moment,' mutters Mrs Audley Jones, meeting Jeanne's eyes in the mirror, 'absolutely the worst time he could have chosen to take early leave.' Jeanne nods, remaining silent. 'A fortnight! If anyone, anyone at all, comes from Onward House,' her voice drops to a whisper, 'they must be sent straight away, and tell them I'll call as soon as I can. Please help me with this earring.'

Jeanne notices two scratches on Mrs Audley Jones's earlobe where the clasp has slipped as it snapped shut.

'Your skin's gone soft,' she says, 'because you never wear them any more.' She eases the clasp gently shut, watching the skin around it swell and redden. 'They're heavy ones, too.'

Mrs Audley Jones waves her hand impatiently and swings her chair round to face Jeanne, her face upturned. Despite her hair, carefully coiled and brushed so smooth it might be made of polished wood, and the blue-stoned jewels bought to match her eyes, Mrs Audley Jones's face looks wild. Jeanne feels in the helpless grip of some catastrophe about to break. 'It'll be all right,' she says hesitantly, unbelieving. She would like to take Mrs Audley Jones protectively into her arms, but this is also something that respect inhibits.

'Last time,' began Mrs Audley Jones, her hand, resting on her knee, jumping a little as if to reach for comfort, or a weapon. 'Last time he forbade me to have anything to do with the Suffrage Movement . . . I said nothing, I made no promises . . . the letters! Jeanne, all the letters that come must be collected before he sees them.' Her voice is so quiet, just an agonised parody of sound. Jeanne nods, meets the eyes staring up at her, and all but drowns in their panic. In the mirror she sees the door behind them opening.

'I'd like to speak to you before we go down to dinner': the voice of the man they both call sir, quiet, but straining to be so. He stands, blocking the light, his head inclined to one side. Jeanne is already moving to the door as Mrs Audley Jones says, 'That will be all.'

The falsity of the calm authority in her voice is, Jeanne thinks, heartrendingly obvious, but then perhaps *he* has never heard her otherwise. However much I would risk for her, I can't do it without her permission: that is being a servant. She shuts the door firmly.

'I understand you have again taken to involving yourself in *charity* work,' says the Admiral, moving towards the dressing table and putting a hand on his wife's shoulder, just as she is about to stand up. Feeling the pressure she slackens her muscles and subsides. Looking at his shadowed face in the mirror, she replies, 'Yes, a little. There is so much that – '

He turns her face towards him with his free hand. 'A home, I understand, for the sheltering of prostitutes.' He plays a moment with the distress visible as twitching and puckering around her mouth. He sees her throat move as she swallows preparatory to speaking – he continues: 'I beg your pardon, the reformation of what is it? *Wayward girls?*' He smiles.

'Indeed I have,' says Mrs Audley Jones, with the last-ditch courage of the cornered, the vehemence of her voice giving her away. 'I consider it a worthy cause; it has the approval of the Bishop of Westminster.'

The Admiral understands her outspokenness for what it is. 'I however, do not approve. It also has the support of those ladies in purple and green.' His hand tips her chin up a little and holds it there. 'It would appear, in addition, that this project has my involuntary support.' His fingers squeeze her jaw. 'Your allowance is for the upkeep of your person and of this house. Both of which are in a state of dereliction.'

'I haven't been well,' she says.

'Don't lie to me,' he says, slapping her just once on the cheek, still holding her face firm; although the slap is a gesture rather than a blow, her skin goes white and then burns. Rage suddenly boils tumultuous inside her, and yet there's no vent for its steam, nothing for it to do except condense into tears.

She jerks herself away at last, out of the light, to hide her face, but that's useless, he knows why she does it, and that's why he lets her. If I am so much afraid of him, she thinks, why do I defy him? All men are the same, I've borne it just because he's away so much.

'Don't treat me like a sailor.'

'I would chastise any man for having dealings with prostitutes. Why should you be different?'

I'm not afraid of him when he's not here, I forget.

'At least show some sense of justice' – I must carry it through, I can't let him crush me.

'Such women taint those who associate with them, morally and socially. Taste for such company must be cut out, wherever it exists – that is why I struck you.'

Mrs Audley Jones sits back in her chair, swamped; the impossibility of useful speech, of altering his view, seems to have made her whole body impotent, and she sways slightly. 'It is men who force women to degrade themselves so,' she says quietly and quickly. 'Marriage is in many respects a similar transaction – ' She stops, afraid. I threw a brick for them, she thinks, hearing her voice in her flesh, defiant, then starts, uncertain for a moment whether she spoke aloud.

'It was best I dealt with this immediately,' he is saying, his voice unchanged, but something about the way he stands indicates a dissipation of his anger. 'Nothing more need be said, I trust. We will, I hope, spend a pleasant few weeks together.'

Something rises to the very top of Mrs Audley Jones's throat and sticks there, hard and huge as a bunched fist. Her husband assumes her stifled silence to be acknowledgement and contrition. 'I will see you downstairs,' he says, just smiling, and without touching her again he closes the door gently with a soft click of the catch that sounds like a surreptitious locking, and then Mrs Audley Jones feels in the hidden bones of her skull that sudden snap of glass, jumping into the razor fragments of a scream.

In the early winter dark, Clara fumbles with matches, washwater from her hands dripping on their heads and stopping them striking. She laughs at herself, dries her hands and begins again. She sets the candle on the ledge of the bed, then begins to unwind the bandages from Michael's eye.

71

'Close your good eye. Look down first,' she says, 'then look up slowly. Tell me if you can see the candle.' She holds the candle in one hand, his damp hand in the other.

'I can't tell if I'm looking up or down!' he says, fear roughening his words, so that, if she didn't know him, she might take them for anger at her. She peers into his eye to see which way it might be looking, but can only see a shadowed socket. Slowly she brings the candle nearer. 'I think it's lighter,' he says when the candle is near enough to cast him the small circle of its brightest light. The muscles of his hands have shrunk, callouses and swellings have softened and sub-sided: they are his hands as she has never seen them before, cut-free, unblistered, lines smoothed out. His nails have grown long, fat crescents of white grace each fingertip. They're hands from a life that might have been.

'Take it away,' he says, 'I can only feel the warmth, no – it's dimmer now.' His voice for a few seconds has a fragile happiness in it, but for Clara, knowing even the 'born-blind' can sense extremes of light and dark, a yearning and a melancholy seem to fill the room like a mist.

'With use your arm will be as good as new,' she says, 'even if the eye . . . Well, one eye sees almost as much as two.' She shuts one of her own to test the truth of what she's said. 'You'll have to turn your neck more, that's all.'

'To judge distances you need two eyes,' he says as if disinterested, correcting her for the sake of accuracy alone. There is a long silence and then Clara, with both eyes shut, begins to stroke his smooth hands with her rough ones. His voice startles her.

'I'll get up on Saturday and begin looking for work on Monday. There's plenty of things one eye will be enough for, gardening perhaps. And if I get better, I'll go back on the tools again, God willing . . .' He too speaks with his eyes closed. Solitary pain, Clara thinks, remembering her operation, cries out for light, for a bright solid world with shadows, something for the eye to grip. How she'd longed to be able to see as she lay there; but shared pain needs darkness so you can't see the

72

other suffering, so the pain can't echo between you endlessly. If there were children, she thinks suddenly, we couldn't have lasted so long on my money with him sick. We'd have had to go to the Board; alone, I've been able to look after him. With this thought the last traces of regret and anxiety about her past disappear like damp creases under a hot iron. She can see the sense now, a big, in-the-future reason she didn't know then, but which takes the pain and the failure and the selfishness out of what she did, and she feels words welling in her as she imagines Michael feels truth and forgiveness and hope rising in him when he steps out of the confessional; she almost speaks but as she hesitates Michael's grip loosens and he falls asleep.

Exhausted, Clara lies on her side next to Michael, who sleeps on his back. Her muscles ache but she's alert; her eyes play at picking out the soft and simple shapes of things in the darkness. She listens as well to the slow endless rain falling and spluttering outside, to the creakings and settlings of the house, to their own breathing, quite separate – for his is shallow and catches every so often, whilst hers is slow and even – yet the rhythms seem paced together, meet and part like two people sharing the same task, like some kind of music. The room seems friendly, part of her. Her muscles untie their knots, seeming almost to sigh in relief as Clara does when she takes off her shoes in front of the stove. Her body presses against Michael's as it loosens. Her thoughts travel in lazy loops, come back slow and heavy like nets full of fish. A hand so supple and sensitive that it cannot, she thinks for a second, be hers, begins to stroke the hollows around Michael's neck and collar-bone. Between her legs a warmth and wetness stretch into an ache, a bubble growing inside her, its walls taut but flexible. The sensation is similar to that she experienced when Marcus Rosenbury put his hand between her legs, but unmarred now by fear, the sensation is exquisite.

The house on Penley Square, so long unused, has burst, suddenly and vividly, into activity. Kitchen maids and a

73

butler have been hired, dust covers removed and whisked into cupboards, mirrors have been polished, fires and lights blaze in every room. The voices of company grow louder every minute that Mrs Audley Jones lingers in her room changing, instant by instant under the influence of panic, into the wife her husband requires. She has added to her jewellery and powdered the invisible slap-mark on her face. She is consumed with worry lest Jeanne has forgotten that the kitchen maid, Elsie, a young woman outspokenly devoted to women's causes, must not wait at table. The past six months have somehow been expelled from her sense of reality; the remnants of them linger to plague her but must be swept away or they will ruin her. She feels light-headed, stupid, takes the stairs slowly as if ill or drunk, but in spite of this she smiles.

'You are looking much better,' her husband says. 'Who is sitting near me at dinner?' She can't remember. 'I'd like to have a talk with that young man, Elverton. Please see to it; I can't bear to be bored at the dinner table.'

'Elverton,' Mrs Audley Jones replies, nodding compulsively.

'You have a little too much powder on your face,' he adds quietly, his hand resting on her arm. Why did she employ that kitchen maid? One part of her seems to goad the other, does things just to disturb. Now is not the time – she offers her hand to the grey-haired man who saw her through the birth of her son and the subsequent period of what he called 'nervous collapse'; the man whose hands reached inside her and touched the mouth of her womb, producing, she remembers, no pain at all but a strange feeling of remoteness and weakness that lasted for some hours afterwards. The same hand eventually administered ether and cut out her womb: she holds that hand now, trusting. Dr Roberts has been her doctor since childhood. He smiles at her, attentive and benign. He does not, she remembers, take alcohol.

'Dr Roberts, would you like some lemonade?'

'My needs have been met already,' he replies, catching her eye and frowning deliberately, turning his face into a caricature of fatherly disapproval. 'Now, my dear, your husband tells me you haven't been well, and he is not the person from whom I should hear such news. Why haven't you called me?'

She blushes from the attention, and the confusion of what is lie and what is truth, and told by whom to what end. Mrs Audley Jones has stood on a platform and addressed five hundred women, but even the memory frightens her now –

'It was nothing much, truly, I had been busy.'

He looks down at her, knowing, indulgent, strong-to-save. 'I shall call tomorrow afternoon, if that's convenient, and we shall see.'

Mrs Audley Jones looks down and sees her dress hangs on her unfilled. She feels a tremor in her hand and grips the mantelpiece. Perhaps she is ill, she thinks, frightened. If I'm cut open again, I'll die.

Mrs Audley Jones feels Elverton's dislike of her, invisible but hard as a panel of glass through which they both have to speak, but through which only he can see. She drops a piece of fish on the tablecloth and knows his eyes linger on it, coolly tactless. Next to her, Dr Roberts is talking to a young woman about water-colours. She feels sudden perspiration on her face, she loses the thread of both the conversations she is supposed to be following. She glances at the Admiral, eating methodically, looking from side to side, waiting to catch Elverton's attention.

'You find it warm?' Elverton asks her loudly.

'Perhaps. My husband is very eager to talk to you tonight.'

'Indeed.' Deliberately, it seems, Elverton refrains from turning to engage the Admiral in conversation. He continues eating, carefully but steadily, glancing at her across the table from time to time. Burning, Mrs Audley Jones directs her attention to the pretence of parting the soft flesh from the skin and bone on her plate.

After dinner, the women settle themselves in the drawing room, and Mrs Audley Jones, having managed to avoid all but polite contact with Mrs Brett, finds they are sitting opposite each other. Although Mrs Brett has her grey hair gathered into a loose knot and wears several strings of pearls, although she is saying in a deep but gentle voice to her neighbour, 'I concern myself a great deal with Human Rights. I am secretary of the Human Rights League,' Mrs Audley Jones is instantly reminded of the last time she saw Mrs Brett, dressed as a man and wiping sweat from her face. When Mrs Brett, turning briefly in her direction, winks, she panics, plunges instantly into a sea of confusion. She is not safe. No, she can rely on Mrs Brett's discretion. They are after all allies if not friends, they have both promised silence. No, she is not an ally, but part of the impossible hallucination that possesses her when her husband is away – in that case, she should not have allowed her own eyelid to fall and linger, unmistakably a gesture of complicity –

'My dear,' says her neighbour, 'you're looking so thin. You haven't been seen for months, literally months.'

'A little off colour perhaps, and much occupied with charity work. What have I missed, Lady Tobitt?' She must have been ill without knowing it. Clearly it's affected both her appearance and behaviour, everyone can see it but her –

'. . . yes, married! With quite unseemly haste, would you believe. We did attend, but afterwards I heard reports – '

Why should he forbid me? Mrs Audley Jones asks herself mildly, and it is as if all evening she has been staring into the snake-green eyes of a hypnotist, sinking, obeying, forgetting, and now, suddenly, the fire has crackled, a book has fallen from the shelf: the contact is broken. There's a leaping fissure in the trance that's swathed and swirled around her since her husband came into her bedroom. Memory of the other life returns with full force, like a dose of sal volatile. That's what's real, not this.

'. . . I dare say they'll be happy enough,' Lady Tobitt smiles at her, exhausted by talk, and no doubt feeling she has earned some return.

'Marriages,' begins Mrs Audley Jones, but she has no plan for the rest of the sentence, 'marriages – for young girls – often have the quality of mirages, don't you think? The contractual nature of marriage is often obscured by the excitement, the enticements – ' Mustn't go too far. Who was I earlier this evening? How does he do it to me?

'Marriage changes a girl from child to woman, overnight so to speak,' interrupts an older woman she does not know, accepting a small cup of coffee.

'Yes,' says Lady Tobitt. 'Without it, we should never grow up.'

'What is it we grow into?'

'Mothers, of course.'

'The transition seems a little abrupt.'

'Juliet married at fourteen.'

'Exactly, the play ends in a tomb.'

'Granted, my dear, few women are completely happy in marriage. But that I think is our nature – '

'But perhaps we are kept childlike; and perhaps our discontent is rational.'

'I am resolutely opposed to divorce, whatever the circumstances. Unless, of course, one found oneself married to a murderer or somesuch.' Lady Tobitt laughs, casting her eyes about the room, a little bored, for they are talking about things she regards as fixed, and about which there is, consequently, very little of interest to be said.

'There are, I should say, similarities in our professions,' the Admiral remarks genially, rubbing blue chalk onto the end of his cue, bending square at the waist over the expanse of green baize. Elverton is silent, watching. '. . . in that both involve, shall I say, strategic thought – ' The Admiral's shot falters and stops just short. Elverton takes his immediately and with success.

'I should say, sir, that the courts of law are more volatile – ' They both follow Elverton's second shot, which cruises purposefully from one end of the table to the other, 'than all the gun boats in the Atlantic.' Clack! with a rumble, Elverton's chosen victim rolls into the hollow grave below the table. He relaxes a little, feeling a satisfactory pattern has been set for the evening.

*

On her way to speak to Janet Lancaster, the lonely young woman who sat next to the doctor at dinner, Mrs Audley Jones passes Mrs Brett, and as she does so, lays her finger momentarily on her lips. Mrs Brett, sitting stiffly because of rheumatism and the reinforcement in her dress, purses her full lips and nods.

The men enter unannounced, walking on solid square-planted black shoes into the seated huddle of women, creating a momentary silence which it is Mrs Audley Jones's function as hostess to fill. She notices that Lord Tobitt is still carrying a billiard cue which he leans surreptitiously behind the door, before folding his hands into the small of his back.

'Talk of the devils,' she says recklessly, thinks perhaps after all she has let her nerves get worn, and counteracts the remark by smiling. Hold on to who I am. Don't give too much away.

'Indeed,' Mrs Brett comes to the rescue, 'what do women ever talk of after dinner but of those they left behind?' Amidst the laughter, Mrs Audley Jones notices her husband, stony-faced. Elverton approaches her.

'I am afraid I may have put your husband out of countenance by venturing to suggest His Majesty's Constabulary are not perhaps the happiest of choices as protectors of morality and decency.'

'Did you venture to suggest who might be more suitable?' she asks icily, and Elverton's shock at the change in her all but shows.

'But of course: the ladies, wives, mothers, daughters.' There's an edge to his voice. 'They have always taken this role upon themselves in private and family matters, and are generally credited with a civilising influence. Some of them even take the law into their own hands: for instance, there are cases where a woman murders her husband and stands to make no monetary gain from it – what can her motive be but a moral one? There are also women who take it upon themselves to throw bricks and even explosives at grave risk to life and liberty. Here again – ' his quick eye catches the backward jump of Mrs Audley Jones's shoulders. Deciding he knows nothing and is merely being sarcastic, she hates him twice over, for his opinions and for having startled her. Deliberately she interrupts, 'I must introduce you, Mr Elverton, to that young lady sitting alone there by the fire.' She rises, propelling him lightly by the shoulder towards Janet. She is twice his age and can afford to be abrupt and domineering; her manner reminds Elverton of that other woman he has never humiliated as he wished.

Mrs Audley Jones knows she will have to wait upstairs in her room for the quiet but peremptory knock of her sea-faring husband, home to partake of his legal rights. There has never been any romance in the encounter. She remembers her conversation with Clara: 'But I don't really mind,' Clara had said; Mrs Audley Jones does mind. Perhaps it's because my womb has been removed. Perhaps I am ill, after all. She will have to lie between the sheets Clara washed and pressed, waiting, memory and intellect cringing once more in antici-pation of her bodily subjection to another's will.

The touch of the blind grows subtle; it is not only from shame and prudence that Clara pulls from Michael's arms to put out the candle. Her desire to tell him her secrets is drenched away by the rising tide of her body's passions, secret so long even from herself; and to touch as if she was blind and deaf seems at this moment to tell more than speech.

Janet is not good-looking, and is unmarried rather than young; in any case Elverton, though capable of discerning female beauty, never succumbs to it.

'Now that we have been introduced, I dare say we must make conversation,' Janet says drily, looking straight back into the fire. She is defending herself because she believes no one would seek her out voluntarily, thinks Elverton, accurately.

'I had hoped we might,' he says, smiling. There is a challenge, too, in pleasing one who resists. 'We share, I guess, a common distaste,' he lowers his voice, 'for occasions such as this.' Janet raises her eyebrows, disdainful and suspicious. Her hairstyle and dress are perfectly adequate to the occasion, yet seem to have been chosen out of duty rather than interest or vanity. One side of her face is flushed from the fire, burned into a kind of life; the other is as evenly pallid as a piece of china. 'What is the root, I am wondering, of yours?'

'You are assuming I acknowledge such a distaste.'

'I was hoping I had met, perhaps, a fellow misanthrope?' he asks smiling. Still Janet hesitates. His successful appearance is at variance with the sentiments expressed.

'You use very elevated words to describe a simple lack of sociability,' she says, not committing herself, but caught.

'Ah, but we – I may presume, Miss Lancaster? – we need some grandeur to decorate what is, after all, a rather austere philosophy, and a little irony also to polish the stones with which we immure ourselves.'

Janet's eyes become huge and shiny as he speaks, salt water collects on the lower rims so that she does not dare to blink.

'Ah yes,' continues Elverton, noticing the precarious pools of misery and shame, 'yet even those little pleasures tend to set the misanthrope yet further beyond the pale.' He stares thoughtfully into the fire, 'An animal exiled from the pen, free, yet hankering for conviviality, even that of fellow sheep. And what are we, after all, but members of a species – '

'Excuse me,' says Miss Lancaster, striding to the door, for the tears have overspilled her restraint, she has mislaid her handkerchief and oh, she's lonely.

Clara has a revelation of her body, a burning dissolution at the centre of which beats a slow, strong pulse, an inwards contraction with a rhythm like rocking, absorbing; delightful and terrible because of what it explains about the past. It has come so late. Herself silent, she hears Michael exhale something between a sigh and a word. Her limbs are weak but she's still afraid she will crush him if she relaxes. This is what should happen: consummation, the word they use even in churches, and all these years she's not known its meaning. Michael too,

80

as innocent as she was; what does he think now of the past years of service offered, as Mrs Audley Jones said, for another's benefit? And why, why now? It must be, she thinks, because she loves him now better than she did, and that is because – because? She cannot answer. She lowers herself gently by his side, an arm and a leg resting on him still, held by dampness and warmth. Mustn't get cold. Perhaps it is because he's sick and she's feared for his life, a spoiled child clutching desperately at what it has disdained as soon as it seems it might be taken away? Because of harder times that bind people each to the other like limed sticks on birds' legs?

'Michael?' She draws up the covers and they hold hands, warmth too scarce to be wasted, fevers to be kept at bay. Her name whispered back. Is it her secret that's made this happen? Is it a reward for audacity and pain endured?

Elverton, now the centre of the little group by the fire, permits himself a little alcohol, thick, old port that sharpens his perceptions even as it makes his face look healthier and more amiable.

'The quality of motherhood will in the end determine the fate of the nation and of the empire,' the Admiral says. His wife has had no children by him, her son died in India before he'd had time to prove himself, or her. Now her womb's gone in any case. 'And not just that of the upper classes, but also the lower.'

'Unfortunately,' interjects Elverton, 'at present often described as the drinking classes.'

The women, proud or anxious according to maternal circumstances, study their hands in their laps.

'Indeed, my friend. Moreover, not only the quality, but also the quantity. We need men in India, in the Antipodes, in all the places over the globe that must be properly administered and policed if savagery is not to be let loose and progress frustrated. At the same time we need workers in factories, on the land. We need good, healthy fellows who'll knuckle under and set to. And we need a damned good navy, and a healthy army.'

'It would seem,' says Mrs Audley Jones, catching a warning in Mrs Brett's eye, but ignoring it, 'that you have no use for us women other than as breeding machines.'

Her husband's face hangs startled for a few seconds, as if he has forgotten who she is, or is unable to decide if she could possibly have said what he heard: her voice after all was quiet and without a trace of hysteria, and it rose at the end like a small child asking a question beyond its years. The seated women still stare at their hands, fiddle with rings. One draws breath to change the subject.

'But Mrs Audley Jones,' says Elverton, patiently, 'what a great use that is. Man's need to multiply, and women's ability to do so, bind society together. Indeed we have a great deal of use for you, and our fate measures exactly according to your harvest, the fruit – ' Elverton puts down his glass, and leaves the sentence incomplete.

'Exactly,' says the Admiral, 'exactly. Woman is the mould that casts the race.'

'Michael, are you awake?' Clara's voice is held quiet, despite the searing mixture of determination, abandonment, fear, that sends her blood racing so that she can feel it even in the tiniest capillaries that normally sleep unnoticed beneath her skin. She will tell Michael what she did, now, but only if he's still awake. She feels as if she's floating, disembodied breath. A few words and then there will be no secret anymore. She's playing a dangerous game, with her new-found contentment and hour-old happiness. There shouldn't have to be secrets. What I did was right.

'Yes', he replies, called back from fuddled netherlands of sleep. Perhaps she wants to give away something she's not used to having . . . but also she imagines the perfection of it, if he were to accept – then again . . .

'Yes', his voice sounds everyday, as if it wasn't dark, as if he's forgotten that tonight his wife, shaking, straddled his body and took him with passion and gentleness as a lover: such a transformation, and now she wants everything else to be as real, as true as her dreams of what might be; her whisper's so full it's shouting, but his 'yes' expects nothing. Clara senses the time is wrong, but she can't stop now. She wants her happiness to be real or not at all.

'Do you remember that time I was sick a few days and didn't do my washing? When we had eels for tea twice in the week?' She has to interrupt his laugh, a shame for it's a laugh soft and enticing as fresh baked bread, but she can't stop now.

'I'd been to see a doctor then. I didn't say, because – because I was afraid that – '

'A doctor, what was wrong?' Out of the corner of her eye she thinks she can see the shape of his face alter, frown. She fixes her eyes steadily on the dark swirling where the ceiling is.

'Promise me you'll not be angry.' He has no idea, not the slightest suspicion. How can she ask him to promise a thing like that, blind?

'I promise that to the Lord every time I pray.' A promise more binding than any made to her. Is anything really different, can it ever be? His quietly spoken phrase curves a hollow of silence after it, and lying apart they each think of how much Michael has to be angry for. His injured eye, work, no work, me, thinks Clara, but Michael's still thinking, 'Without pride I say it, but I could have been not just a carpenter or a joiner but a cabinetmaker; with a union at the back of them they'll always do all right. I've got it in me, but now I'm not even Mr Holden's mate but a gardener, a one-eyed loafer.' When he does think of what Clara did to their child, the words that come to his mind from force of habit grown to be second nature are, 'And I've no children, and I wanted them.' He's not forgotten, but he doesn't remember. There's no shortage of food for anger, Clara thinks, in my life too.

'What was the matter? How did you pay? Why should I be angry? You should have said – '

She can't help but laugh, a falling-downstairs laugh, all bumps and creaks: should have said!

'A lady I know paid the money. I wasn't ill. I went to have an operation called a termination.' Her heart beats fast but

83

incredibly light. There are only two directions her life can take now. It depends on him. Alternately she imagines each of them, the desired and the feared, twenty times before he replies.

'What's that?' There is a tightness in his voice as if he half knows the answer, knows at any rate it's something bad.

' – womb –' Clara mumbles, the words coming from outside of her and taking clumsy shape, 'like terminus. But it's not the same, it's not alive, it really isn't.' Her voice dribbles to nothing and silence grows like a deadly bubble, inexorable, stretching to encompass and poison more and more of their lives. He draws a long breath between his teeth, and Clara begins turning to look at him face on.

'Don't,' he says, and her movement petrifies, one elbow dug into the mattress, her neck swung so that his face is only just out of comfortable sight. He's crossing himself, and the faint, wet sounds of his tongue and lips mean that he's praying silently, eyes shut, mouth shaping words – she's seen him do it a thousand times. Wait. A word slips accidently into sound: 'Jesus', and hearing it, Clara also hears hope running out: a dry, rushing sound, like tea being poured from its packet into the caddy, she feels the lightening, slackening under her fingers, and in a matter of seconds nothing remains but a scattering of spilled dust. It's all gone, all thrown away, and there's such a sense of loss, a sudden blenching like when the knife's pulled from the wound and the pain and bleeding are about to begin. All this, the weeks of growing contentment, the just revealed night-flower of bodily expressed love and the knowledge it hints at, a sudden edifice of dreams: all this has rushed backwards away from her, fast as a train, just a rush of air, now vacuum, all gone.

'Oh Lord,' he says, 'give your servant strength', his body rigid. Clara feels hers, too, gradually stiffen. It's all gone. This he'll not forgive. This cancels out everything.

Elverton refuses a cab; he always takes a walk at night. The Admiral clasps his hand firmly, hoping to impress as he's been impressed. 'You must have lunch with me before I leave.'

Elverton nods gravely. 'I trust your wife's health will improve.'

The Admiral is shorter than Elverton, but much more solidly built. His features, stern and bitter-looking, seem at the same time curiously guileless as he looks into the crisp, blank face of the younger man. He wants to tell him about the countries he has seen, and the way his fleet is disciplined and co-ordinated, and how this is the exact way the world ought to be governed; he wants to tell him that when he leaves the service he will stand for Parliament – he presses Elverton's hand again as if the pressure will intimate some of this, hint at least at weightiness, significance, presence and solidity. He would like Elverton to consider him rather as a son, he imagines, might respect a worthy father.

Upstairs Mrs Audley Jones begins to shake as she undresses herself. She's told Jeanne not to wait up for her, but wishes she hadn't. I hate him, she thinks, I hate him. Nerves, nerves.

Michael begins to weep and Clara feels bitter at the privacy of his grief: no words, not even sobs, just a steady procession of mean little tears. Tight and hard as pebbles, men's tears, but like all things extracted with difficulty, valued high, higher, she knows, than the commoner tears women cry.

Ignorance and forgetting are Michael's only defences. Now, knowledge has burst through and it's all happening this instant so can't be forgotten, and it wells up, volcanic, strong enough to push aside even prayer, that gentle envelope swaddling that's protected him over the years from many emotions, but most especially from pain. That his wife Clara killed his first child in its bed and has now aborted his second become indistinguishable events, doubly vivid. He lies rigid only because his fretful muscles don't yet know where to carry him.

The horror of it, to kill a child! He thinks of a human-faced creature older and more fully formed than the born girl-child

85

ever was, and then he sees it bathed in blood. Murdered! The image, in his mind's eye, mesmerises and terrifies him. He sees Clara, younger than she is, her skin pink and white, creamy as it's never been. The vision taunts him: she has killed. The two images resist as they move towards each other: the beautiful Clara, the dead child, straining against union, with miserable victories and losses along the way like two limbs pitted in combat. All of a sudden, resistance ceases, Clara stands by her work: his wife killed his children. An urge to strike her, to turn and break what has broken his peace with the world, and his meagre hopes, rears itself like a nightmare figure about to beat Michael himself. Michel flails and grasps for his Saviour, mumbles His name and makes the sign of the Cross. But it is as if God has disappeared or turned his back, his prayers are sound only. Michael, for the first time in years, is on his own with the full iniquity of the world, Clara, himself; his only thought now is that he must reach God, must see a priest.

He fumbles with his overjacket and trousers, aware of Clara obediently lying still. Waves of hatred rush through him; he would like to beat her, murder her. His fingers and limbs are enfeebled by the weeks of lying in bed. Getting dressed is a race against himself and time.

'Get out of this house of the devil' – but the words aren't strength enough – 'to the house of God.' He feels sure that there a great calm will fall upon him, a silence, and he will hear inside him a clear voice telling him what he should do. The Lord has only disappeared in his pain, as a flame does in daylight; if he is calm then He will return. He closes the door with a push: it only just shuts, despite the effort the sudden movement cost him. Tears come to his eyes, it's so awful what she's done, it can't be wiped out, ever, and it seems it's partly him that's done it: because she's his wife, because he lived with her, knowing. It's a thing so awful that no one speaks of it, it's the worst crime he can think of, killing the unbaptised innocent, and it has happened between his four walls, it has slept between his sheets. No priest would absolve her. She has

86

not ever been a truly godly woman, he has failed in his duty to make her one. He has lived with the devil, a she-devil who only that night has roused him with temptations of the flesh and lied to him with her tenderness.

Breathing hard, Michael stumbles down narrow streets feeling the walls with his hands to steady himself. He sees things that are not real. He thinks he is going to confession; everything is very muddled. Cold gets behind the bandage around his eye. God! The church is a mass of dark in the dimness. Its gates are locked. He begins to run.

Constable Edmonds crosses Lambeth Bridge at regulation pace for the third time. He's not yet quite comfortable with his new work. At the quietest time of the night, between three and half-past four: the time when all the trains have stopped, and the markets haven't yet begun, when mists precipitate themselves and he can hear the chaffing of his trousers and shoes, he, the watcher, feels watched. He carries himself particularly upright for the benefit of the imaginary, invisible watcher, and turns to look behind him much more often than required. Although his feet ache, this last circuit takes him as much as fifteen minutes less than the previous one.

The river slops and sulks, sucks and smells. Edmonds peers over the side of the bridge to check for suicides or objects floating in the water; looks behind him; counts out his steps and tries to slow them down. Suddenly he hears a woman singing, the sound sweeping, drunken, generous, but he can see no one: she must be just hidden by the hump of the bridge. He can't make out the words at all. It might be hymns, it might be bawdy. He waits quietly, there's nothing to be afraid of. He sees the woman leaning on the parapet singing out over the water that stretches and smoothes the sounds before bearing them off into the last moments of darkness. Edmonds too leans on the parapet, about a hundred yards away, facing the river but looking sideways at the woman.

It's Lizzie, the woman in green, who's singing. She sings only when she's had a lot too much and when she's sad enough not to care. When she hears singing at Music Hall or church Lizzie sits quiet but feels the sung sounds tugging at her own vocal chords, the way half-lost memories pull at thoughts. She wishes she could sing, knows secretly she can, that she could have been a singer, not a slut, and then she's filled with regret and pity for the voice caged up within her, and all tunes seem sad. Now as she sings she patches the tunes and words together from remembered bits and what seems right:

> Through the vale of life
> Oh, where, Oh where've you gone –

The tempo changes frequently but the tone is the same, as if all tunes, marches, laments, jigs, and ballads, have been painted over with the same lugubrious colour.

> No never, no never
> he said no never
> you cannot be my wife
>
> for I am lost
> all on the wide wide seas
> for I have lost
> the treasures of my soul –

Edmonds, momentarily entranced by the half-sense words and the voice's early-morning echo, pulls himself together: the woman is blind drunk.

> For if yer face is yer fortune
> lady you're in need of relief
> if yer face is yer fortune
> best put it in the bank –

Tears stream down Lizzie's face as she sings. There is no need for Edmonds to creep up quietly; her songs blind her to the world.

> All those might-have-beens

sings Lizzie, the words her own now,

just might have been grand.

She breaks off singing to swear loudly, 'Bleeding sodding joke that is!'

'What are you doing here at this time of night?' asks Edmonds. Lizzie laughs. She's seen his face before. He recognises her as soon as the light catches her face; she's wearing the same green dress.

So that no light will show under her door, Mrs Audley Jones turns out her gas as soon as she hears her husband on the stairs, and sits motionless on the edge of her bed. The steps pause outside her door.

'Christine!' His voice seems loud enough to wake the dead. She sits tight, willing the room to silence. There's not even a ghost of light since both shutters and the thick winter curtains have been drawn; even the acute surface of the mirror is blind; the dark is darker than the darkness behind closed eyes. Mrs Audley Jones hears her husband walk briskly away from her door, and a feeling of exhausted triumph slackens her body as if she had fought him off with shouting and blows. She feels she could sit forever in the dark that's protected her, but when she's quite sure he must be sleeping, she turns on the gas just enough to make a pool of semi-light to write in.

Dear girls, she begins, It seems such a long time until I shall see you all again, but I think of you daily, and imagine you all conquering your typing machines, letter by letter . . .

The half-light makes imagining Onward House even easier: the dormitory with its twenty beds and screens, the cool basement kitchen that's sometimes a classroom. She thinks of the 'girls': the pinched, mistrustful features of the youngest, Emma Bendow, when she first arrived, now filled out and proud of herself. Mrs Audley Jones remembers them mostly by their eyes, all different; together, like a sea that can change suddenly with a breath of feeling wind. She's tasted the exhilaration of work with a purpose and hope, and seen the same pleasure catch in Onward House like measles. The din of twenty typewriters excites her: clatter bang bang, quicker than a heartbeat and quicker still every week, the dragged rip of finished sheets pulled out. She'd like to have a print shop as well; she knows absolutely nothing of publishing but she can hear the strong rhythm of the presses, can see stacks of sheets pouring off to be sorted and bound by girls in calico aprons. Dreams. But perhaps you can do anything if you really try: Onward House, Printers for the Female Suffrage Movement. All our employees are female. But who would teach them printing, collating, binding? Stick with the possible. Mrs Audley Jones finishes her letter, seals it unaddressed in a plain envelope, and puts it by her bed for Jeanne to deliver in the morning.

A grey, querulous dawn leaks into the sky, and Lizzie feels a hundred years old, pains and dullness settling on her sudden as dew-fall.

'Come on, sonny,' she says to Edmonds, heart not in it, heart not anywhere, 'after a pretty walk by the river, you can't take a girl to the lock-up. And there wasn't no one about to disturb the peace of, except your good self. Let's be friendly.'

'And what would you mean by that?' says Edmonds.

'What I say.' Lizzie's wary, weary, wanting no more than to fall asleep as she walks, and to wake never, or in the next world. 'Can't be any worse than this dog end of a life,' she mutters. Edmonds' fingers dig into her arm, which is already straining in its socket because of difference in their heights. Edmonds is to be married in three weeks' time.

'One thing's for certain, you're up to no good,' he says.

Lizzie's thinking she'll have to try and run for it. To one side the river, glinting now with the just-yellow sun; a small lighter is coming out into the centre stream. To the other side, small lanes and alleys are still completely shadowed.

'Haven't I seen you somewhere before?' she asks. Edmonds' grip falters, but not enough.

'Would your wife like to know where it was I saw you before?' she says in a theatrical whisper, just as a small sandy-haired man bursts out of one of the alleys. A bandage around his head holds a patch over one eye, the uncovered eye is raw-rimmed, twitches and stares.

'Constable! My wife's done child-murder – what shall I do?' the man shrieks, stopping dead to do so, crossing himself, a tear hangs waiting on the inner corner of his eye. Lizzie realises she's free, and runs. Edmonds stands rooted, unable to choose.

'I know where to find you, and I will,' he shouts into the alleys that hide her.

.4.

Clara's alone in the thin hours of morning. Why is it that in miserable solitude thoughts and feelings suddenly find the words they've lacked, just when there's no one to say them to? Misery waits under the floorboards like a rat with its own secret hole. If I could find it I'd block it up good and proper; after all, what's the sense in crying? It's done and told and look what's happened; you ought to laugh, you ought to laugh. Where's he gone? He won't come back. Fallen down in the street like a drunk, drunk with rage and pain, oh, what've I done? It's in the past, what I did, and all for the good. 'Your tongue will find you out,' Ma used to say. Telling your own secrets, far worse than other people's. Doesn't anyone else have secrets and misery-rats under the floor? But they don't tell. What can happen now? Life's like a cage you can't get out of, but I've always wanted to live. They say there's always hope. Where? You're meant to tell the truth, but least said the better. Can't blame him, I knew what he was like, but I hoped. Luck's in the blood, or not. Written in your hand some say. Hope sometimes grows again, slowly, like hair, but you lose it in the end. But Christ, I've as much right to weep as him! Clean hands, Christ's got, like a judge, but young.

Dry-eyed, she thinks with longing of something like the easy way water runs off shiny leaves in a storm, and tries to remember her mother, but she can't, dreading, perhaps, the questions she'd ask. Always when she's alone the words grow stronger and stronger inside their fragile shells, tap tap they never quite break out, and she never knows what they might have been, the real truth. Telling of her abortion was perhaps only the beginning of what Clara might have revealed to Michael, but now it's gone.

She waits. His saw, axe and hammer as well as his clothes mean that he will have to come back. Another hour passes, and Clara begins to feel the first prickings and itchings of hope; carefully, she murders them.

Michael knows he'll have to go home; knows that the police, sooner or later, will visit his house to see his wife and that they'll take her away, and that Mrs Audley Jones – he's sure she must be 'the lady I know'. He will have to stay in the room and pretend she isn't there. It's impossible to imagine. He could tell her, give her time to get away. Justice. Justice. A stream of prayers intersperse Edmonds' questions and Michael's answers: oh Lord give me strength – it's raining in his head and the stream must flow faster and faster – forgive us all our sins – until it's a torrent that will bear him along untouchable.

If he had found a priest first, he'd perhaps not have spoken to Edmonds. He gives Mrs Audley Jones's name and address: 'One of those suffragettes, she is, it was one of them that got that girl's face all cut.' Marriage is a sacrament that cannot be dissolved. Abortion is murder, is a mortal sin even if the rope is spared. A spouse's evidence is not admissable in court, except under some circumstances; neither is hearsay: there will be a period of waiting while investigations take place. Michael's blind eye throbs in its hot darkness.

'Frightful business this, sir,' says Edmonds. 'You've only got to read the papers to see it's happening more and more: wives poisoning their husbands, murdering their little babies, taking their own lives: small wonder the world's the way it is if women do such things the same as men.'

'I don't know what to do.' The torrent of holy words in his

head had dwindled to a trickle: stranded, his good eye stares, begging, at Edmonds, round and silly as a lost child's, that can't remember its name and address.

'You did right to report it,' says Edmonds. 'It's got to be stamped out, or where will it end? And there's those suffragettes shouting and heckling outside the House of Parliament itself, chaining themselves up, throwing bricks and even bombs. The law needs stiffening up. D'you know, the law says that if a woman kills her own child while she's giving birth, before it's quite out of her, there's no crime she can be tried for? You'd not think it was possible in a Christian country, but it is, the devil. Women get away with murder. In this job you see it all, and it's not a pretty sight . . .'

Edmonds talks because he's excited. The truth is that the most startling thing he's seen since he joined the force is a woman without her skirts, and tonight this has landed in his lap, just like that.

'. . . Why, a respectable chap like yourself, a religious man, wouldn't believe the half of what goes on in this city.' He's officially off duty now, but in no mood to go back to his lodgings. 'And quite right too – but the trouble with that' – he's repeating overheard conversations of his superiors – 'the trouble with that is that the average man, especially the average gentleman, as is one of the twelve sitting on a jury, simply cannot believe anyone capable of committing such terrible crimes as are committed, and particularly not when the accused wears a skirt and sheds a few tears. So they ignore the evidence and acquit. You look like you could do with something to set you up, Mr Riley. I know a good place for breakfast, and I'll buy it for you if you like.'

One in pieces, half-blind and fumbling for the thread of a prayer, the other swelled with triumph and expectation, they go for hot, sweet tea, salty bacon pink and thick on slabs of bread fried in the drippings of the pan. It's truly morning now, the sun streaming unusually bright, more like spring but for the length and darkness of the shadows.

*

Mrs Audley Jones comes to breakfast late, and the Admiral has already started his meal. He seems cheerful.

'Can't get used to shore hours,' he says. 'By now, I would've been up for – ' he consults the clock, squinting at it as if it were perched on a distant horizon, 'three hours and forty-five minutes.'

Mrs Audley Jones, although very hungry on rising, finds that a few mouthfuls fill her up; any more, she knows, will cause her stays to press too hard into her abdomen. It's best not to eat and drink at the same time. He was reading *The Times* when she came in; now he folds it together with the comment 'shocking', but does not offer it, merely transfers his attention to his wife as she sips a cup of warmed milk.

'Really took to that Elverton chap,' he says. 'He'll go far.'

Boredom, as well as fear, is the enemy; it lines her mind, as the milk does her stomach, coating sensations of discomfort, discontent and wanting, so that they are less recognisable. She must take pains to remember all the things she thought of in the middle of the night: surrounded by furniture, and watched over by her husband, it seems difficult; she can feel herself shrinking inside. Leave him? Impossible, the courts can compel her return, the 'restitution of conjugal rights'. Now that Onward House is bought, she has no money of her own. It's only two or three weeks, and then he'll be gone again. But when he retires from duty, whispers the relentless night-voice, what will you do then?

'. . . the opera tonight, I think, and a drive in the afternoon. You've been too secluded.'

'Very well.' Again her cold voice has to be counteracted with a smile: the venom seems to spurt out like sprung leaks despite her knowing it's better to say nothing at all than even to hint at offence.

'I think you keep too small an establishment when I am not here.' She says nothing.

While she is dressing Dr Roberts calls: it seems the Admiral has invited him to see her, and to lunch afterwards. He comes to her room, unannounced, this familiarity granted by surgical intimacy and the fact that he attended her mother at her birth. He sits heavy and inappropriate among the flowered cloths and spindly furniture.

'Thank you for calling,' she says, 'but really, so far as my health is concerned, there is no reason at all.'

Like Jeanne Biggs, the doctor has contradictory orders from husband and wife; he, however, will always obey the Admiral, not only because it is he who pays his fees, but also because he credits a man's judgement as superior to a woman's and believes that a woman, though she should be treated with all possible outward respect, is under her father's or husband's command.

'I think there is some cause for concern. Your face is very drawn, and you are thin. You may have a nervous condition. Allow me – '

He takes her pulse. She knows that for some reason it began to race when he entered the room. They go over to the window and he looks into the pupils of her eyes, which begin to water from keeping them unblinking in the light. He says nothing for a while, then, 'Are you happy? Is there anything on your mind?'

'Perfectly,' she says, knowing in her bones that conceal-ment is all.

'Your husband is often away. You must be lonely, you must miss – the . . . the companionship of marriage. Any woman would.'

She does not answer. When they turn from the window, her husband is standing in the doorway. Dr Roberts smiles, and they shake hands heartily.

'Your wife is at a dangerous point in a woman's life,' he begins without further preliminaries. 'To some extent all women suffer at this age, but things may be worse in your wife's case as she has a history – she is not stable – and needs care. She needs to lead a regular life, with company and entertainment to prevent her from becoming melancholy.'

'I am not normally melancholy more than the world gives me occasion to be,' interrupts Mrs Audley Jones. The doctor turns to look at her.

'Precisely,' he continues, voice and face soft and soothing. 'A woman situated as well as yourself has no cause at all for melancholy: the world has treated her well, and many of her sisters in less advantageous situations would be understandably envious of her. These feelings are part of a slight nervous disorder associated with the middle time of a woman's life. There is no cause for concern,' he turns back to the Admiral, 'provided that you take steps to ensure a daily life busy in the pursuit of diversion and pleasure, a diet nourishing but not heating: milk custards, and a little chicken breast, for instance, rather than red meats or thick broths . . .'

By the time they leave, Mrs Audley Jones is shaking with rage at being reduced to nursery status: milk custards, and you should think of others worse off than you. You should be grateful to your husband and obedient: that's his treatment for my supposed sickness! But she's also badly frightened. There was an air of conspiracy about the two of them, their whiskers and starch-white shirts, their smells of tobacco and bergamot: there is no way she could have made them listen to her, and if they decide she's ill, then as far as the world is concerned, ill she will be. It occurs to her that if her husband wants her confined, he has only to ask Roberts: she's heard of such things. The visit, she's sure, is a calculated threat.

Even at such short notice, a light bouillon followed by coddled eggs has been prepared for Mrs Audley Jones's lunch. The eggs, half-set, quiver on the china plate, two blobs of yellow amidst an amorphous, heaving whiteness. She is torn between her instinct to refuse the food imposed on her and her estimation that to refuse or pick will be construed as evidence of her nervous condition. The matter is decided for her in that she cannot swallow. She sits, like a temperamental child who will be severely punished for its trifling defiance, yet leads itself inexorably on, as if to provoke injustice. The lack of dignity in her situation makes her face burn, her palms sweat: she sits silently and watches the two men eat cutlets and peas as if nothing had happened.

'Colleague of mine visited Africa just after the war,' Dr Roberts is saying, 'says the climate is the unhealthiest he's ever met, and it's no wonder the people are so peculiarly ill developed and so little resistant to disease. The climate has held evolution back thousands of years . . . The women there in particular are little removed from animals in Darwinian terms. Of course, medicine could relieve some of the symptoms, but it can't improve the stock – '

Mrs Audley Jones, staring at the white and yellow eggs, white and yellow crustless bread and butter, knows suddenly that she has nothing to lose. She might as well join the others on hunger strike in jail, the martyrdom she's always guiltily shrunk from. She might as well let herself be manhandled into prison and spat on by officers of the Law as sit on the brink of tears staring at a plate of poached eggs. Indeed, she would rather, if she has to be circumscribed and humiliated and starved, that it was public and for some good reason, with some aim and sense of hope in it, not this awful private submission that could never be more than exactly that: submission. She might as well give up all pretence, get up from the table this instant and take a cab to Onward House, and see if they dare –

But, oh yes, they will dare. They will lock her up as mad. They will drug her and carry her away, if necessary; they will if they want to – She is caught, her heart plucked by both bravery and fear, and knowing she cannot belong to both.

The eggs are lifted away, and a portion of hot treacle tart served to all of them.

'You must take some nourishment at midday, m'dear,' says the doctor in parenthesis as he elaborates on the iniquities of bribery and corruption amongst the new breed of native civil servants in India. He raises one tangled eyebrow as he speaks to her, and drops it abruptly when he turns back to the Admiral.

The two large and one small portions of treacle tart are

steaming untouched as one of the servants, hired for the duration of the Admiral's leave, knocks and enters the dining room, walks up to the Admiral and whispers in his ear.

'Who? What on earth?'

The Admiral stands up, face enraged; the slamming of three doors is heard, and then silence. Mrs Audley Jones is surprised, but insulated from curiosity by her own present humiliation and the effort to think her way through it. She seizes the opportunity to quit the table, leaving Dr Roberts calmly beginning to eat.

Jeanne is waiting for her at the bottom of the stairs, and follows her striding up them. They shut the bedroom door. To Mrs Audley Jones, the well-dusted room looks impossible, unreal, because it doesn't fit the circumstances that threaten it: prison cell, lunatic asylum.

'They're trying to turn me into an invalid,' she throws at Jeanne, standing with every muscle pitched at its tightest, as if to prove her robustness. Her voice is full of the contempt and hatred she has not yet dared to vent on the men downstairs. 'I can't bear it. I'm leaving immediately for Onward House. I don't care what happens. I've put up with it far too long.'

She turns abruptly, and jerks open the drawers of her dressing table, rifling them for jewellery. 'Even this probably belongs to him by law. A woman is nothing – ' she slams a drawer shut, 'nothing at law, as elsewhere: there's a bit of gallantry, chivalry, but no rights, no commonsense justice – ' She slams another drawer and the little crashes and falling noises from inside the dressing table suddenly seem very loud. She realises Jeanne hasn't spoken since they met on the stairs.

'Jeanne?'

'I think you should know, Madam – ' the voice comes immediately behind her. Raising her eyes she can see Jeanne's small shiny hands in the mirror, each one thrust halfway up the opposite sleeve. 'It was the police that came to see the Admiral – ' *The brick*, thinks Mrs Audley Jones, 'and I heard them in the hall. They said "It concerns some allegations made against your wife".'

'Oh.' Leaving seems useless now: if they want her for that they'll find her. She lowers herself on to a footstool, her back leaning against the dressing table. A few minutes ago she was eager to be imprisoned as a martyr to a cause: now the thought of what is to come collapses her. 'I thought this might happen, but not with him here, I never thought of that.' Her laughter is feeble, and they both know it is the signal of weeping to come.

'What is it all about?' Jeanne asks timidly, crouching down a little abruptly and awkwardly, aware that the movement is, under the circumstances, a sign that respect will no longer inhibit her. She puts her hand on Mrs Audley Jones's shoulder and grips it firmly, as if physically to pull someone back from a trance. 'What is it?'

'Jeanne, it's a secret: I threw a brick through some shop windows in Oxford Street. A brick with "Votes for Women" on it. It was in the papers. It was – marvellous, but someone was hurt.'

For a second Jeanne looks very shocked and solemn, and then they are both laughing, sitting on the floor and laughing, half at the funny side and half at the respect that's fled, laughing loud enough that nothing matters at all. Then the Admiral walks in.

Even after Jeanne's been sent away, Mrs Audley Jones feels the memory of that laugh swimming inside and twitching at her lips, irrepressible. She looks into her lap to conceal it.

'That was the Constabulary,' he says, 'I've bought you some time. Or rather, Dr Roberts has.'

She says nothing, feeling the laugh breathe its feeble last.

'They wanted to question you immediately, but he said you were in no condition to be interrogated.'

The laugh is dead.

'I'll get Elverton on to it, if I have to: this must not get out. That is the first thing.' He moves closer. 'Get up!' He pulls her up by the elbows. 'There is not language strong enough to describe what you have done. A crime against Nature, the law, God and your own sex.'

'Don't exaggerate, and let me go.' She doesn't struggle, however, feeling that that would only humiliate her and enrage him.

'Exaggerate! It is a most unnatural kind of murder and you are charged with being an accessory to it – '

Oh Clara, Clara: the hugeness of her misapprehension, the folly of her laughter, tower over her, more overwhelming even than the man gripping her, his face pinched and flushed by hatred and fury rising second by second to the point when, she knows, he will strike her.

Clara doesn't speak when Michael comes in, but smiles a little and sets bread on the table. It's past their dinnertime. He looks dirty and very ill. If only she could undo what she did – or undo the telling . . . Blinded by pity, she sets a kettle to boil considering desperately that she might tell him what she said in the night was not true. Her tongue and body yearn to express overpowering regret, but she holds herself silent and moves slowly about the room because she has no idea what he is thinking, and what effect her words may have on the unsteady figure trying to sit upright on the bed. Slowly the room fills with steam, wet whiteness that fuddles sight, the faintly metallic smell that slips down the throat, making the lungs seem to puff out with nothing inside.

He refuses food. Careful as a dancer who mustn't make a sound, Clara removes from the table what she set there. She's done no washing this morning and the money's needed, but the noise and the violent activity seemed impossible. She sits at the table. The act that has caused this pain-strangled silence seems unreal. Hours pass; the fire's out.

'Shall I bathe your eye, and put a new bandage on it?' she says, very, very quietly, so as not to shock.

'No.'

She hears him pick at his bootlaces, the shift and creak of the bed. Quiet swamps the room again. Clara stays sitting at the table. Outside, she can hear the other tenants taking their turns at the water closet. Upstairs, Mrs Dickens' sixth cries, is cuffed, and cries again.

*

'There's no way out of it, they found the damn doctor's address in your papers. They had a warrant. And there was money out of our account the day before. You're no better than a murderess. Understand, I am doing this not for your sake, but in order to prevent scandal. I'll do all I can to prevent it getting to court; however, if it does, you will plead "not guilty". It is Clara Riley's word against yours. I am seeing the surgeon tomorrow to see if something can be arranged. I'll take advice from Elverton. I'm extending my leave indefinitely. You will not leave the house. All this will cost me a great deal of money.'

Inspector Garvey shakes Elverton's hand with genuine enthusiasm.

'Good on you, sir, I was on tenterhooks until the very last minute.' Elverton, silent, smiles thinly. He's exhausted. He's brought Garvey's problem case to a successful conclusion: the stock-broker's wife has been sentenced to hang (though, as Garvey pointed out, the way things are these days, it's bound to be commuted) for poisoning him with arsenic. The missing motive: an imagined mistress, jealousy.

'I always say, if there's to be slander – scandal, it's best scandal about the dead. But I never thought, Mr Elverton, sir, that it could be done with so few words. Mr Elverton, you're an artist!'

Garvey has Elverton by the elbow: an ill-fleshed arm, inert, unsweating flesh that repels him slightly. Alive in the mind, half-dead in the body, he thinks, letting go, taking breath and considering whether or not this might be the moment to bring before Elverton his new problem case: Rex versus Audley Jones, Penfold and Riley.

'Like a word with you, sir – business,' he whispers loudly as they reach a staircase, stopping to speak. Elverton however continues, taking the steps evenly and looking straight ahead into empty air.

'There's no time like the present,' he says, and smiles broadly to himself.

'You seem, sir, remarkably collected for a man in your position,' the Admiral says, unable to meet Dr Penfold's eyes, and looking instead at his hands: square-cut nails and thick fingers that have been in women's private parts. The man revolts him. Dressed as a gentleman, sitting straight-backed and systematically dealing with a plate of food, as if nothing had happened. The Admiral wants his co-operation; his original thought was that the man was unscrupulous scum but he must use tact and flattery to buy him off. Now, incensed, he finds himself saying:

'A man standing to lose not only his criminal but also his legitimate living – ' Penfold's knife and fork hesitate, then resume their course.

'There was some cause for concern,' he says, 'but I have taken advice, and now feel quite confident.'

'What advice? What do you mean?' Both are muttering their words, although the room is entirely private.

'Did you want something from me?' counters Doctor Penfold. His face is flushed, his small eyes flicker from the plate before him to the Admiral's face.

'You monster,' says the Admiral, 'you're no better than a savage: massacring the innocent and giving women the means to damn themselves in debauchery.' He stuffs his mouth shut with a forkful of food, tasting nothing.

'As to whether a foetus has, or has not, a soul, or even life, that is a philosophical question first asked by the Greeks and not yet answered conclusively. The question as to whether or not women should be able to prevent birth is also unresolved. Even the Roman Church appears to have modified its opinion from time to time. I am not a moralist, though I see no benefit to anyone in the existence of unwanted children. I simply supply a service which is in great demand. Are you sure there is nothing you want of me? If so . . . '

The Admiral swallows hard. 'I want my wife out of this.'

'I'm not surprised.'

Silence. The two men take brandy glasses, and stand by the fire, the doctor appearing to be lost in tranquil thought. After a while, he says, 'I see no insurmountable difficulty in that. Listen: in the terms of the present Abortion Act, it's an offence for a person to abort a woman who is with child, and also an offence for a woman to attempt to abort herself; there is room for manoeuvre here. What happened in the case of Clara Riley is that she, in the terms of the Act, used an instrument on herself. But she succeeded only in causing lesions, bleeding and pain. These symptoms became obvious to your wife who, alarmed but of course unaware of the cause, brought her to me. I, in order to prevent her death, had no choice but to finish the business. In this way Mrs Riley is entirely responsible for her own miscarriage.'

The Admiral sits down heavily. 'What are your terms?' he asks. 'Who gave you your advice?'

'A young man possessing a highly developed mind and, like myself, little interest in morality. There are no terms. I provide a service, at present illegal, but I am not a blackmailer. You, I trust, are aware that you yourself are in no position to be one either?'

At dusk Michael is still sleeping and Clara takes her fourth wash to the yard. It seems very peaceful, a clear winter sky and the big white sheets billowing gently in a breath of wind. Indoors she has pounded and wrung as gently as possible in order not to disturb Michael's sleep. Several times she's stood and looked at his sleeping face, motionless and smooth as those of the painted saints in church. His sleep seems magical; she almost believes that when he wakes all will be well again. She drifts in a feeling of weak joy as after the crisis of fear. The sheets make a noise that must, she thinks, be like the sails of ships that float on the sea she's never seen.

The yard door breaks open, the bottom catching and scraping on stones. A second violent push wrenches its hinges from the half-rotten post; it crashes to the ground. Two policemen stride across the yard, parting the sheets and sweeping them aside. One sheet falls to the ground, its pegs snapping off and flying through the air. Clara rushes to pick it up, and Edmonds catches at her arm.

'Come on, leave that alone.'

'You're under arrest,' says the other constable. Clara and Edmonds are tugging at the muddy sheet. As the second man grasps her from behind, it splits clean across the weave with a sound that seems, in the still chill air, like the tearing apart of something much stronger than mere cloth. Clara joins in its scream, and then begins to fight.

Her foot flings backwards into a knee, her fingers fly to a face, no nails to scratch with but she grabs handfuls of cheek, sweat and spittle; she spits and spits, screams, tears at braids and badges; a whistle blows, she jerks and twists her waist; suddenly free, her legs kick high as a gaiety girl's and the yard spins round, all bits of sheet and faces, but she's free; she doesn't think to run, she jerks up Edmonds' leg, straining against it until the sudden slackening: and he's down; she throws herself on him, pulling flesh and cloth alike. Now there's six officers, maybe more. She's pinned against the yard wall, a noise in her head goes on and off. A bucket of rain-water slaps into her chest, drenching her dress and dribbling down her legs. 'I – ' she begins, but looking at them and the yard, a battlefield festooned with empty lines and twisted filthy sheets, she stops. Her hands are locked behind her. Edmonds, with blood on his face, is laughing at an uneasy pitch. Surrounded, Clara is taken from her yard. Behind her, a single remaining sheet fills lazily with the wind, and Michael her husband, with his holy waxwork face still sleeps, flat on his back in the deserted kitchen, laundry, bedroom, with the deal table, and smiling-monkey Pope, the secret store of scented soap, and fresh air blowing in through the open door to make the day's steam settle into wetness.

Elverton sits alone in a box at the Haymarket Theatre. Below him, tiny figures prance and jabber, and the scarcely visible massed audience giggles, catches its breath, holds itself still as the ladies prepare to weep. A red-jacketed man on crutches speaks full-faced to the audience; behind him a woman crouches and weeps silently. 'I have fought in great wars, seen starvation and many other faces of death. But these evils in foreign lands can be matched . . . ' Elverton, his eyes still following the puppet-like figures below, reviews the three people in the case of Rex versus Penfold, Riley and Audley Jones, to whose interests and desires in the matter he has become privy. There's Garvey who wants them all to suffer; there's Admiral Audley Jones who wants his wife and himself saved from scandal at any financial or moral cost; and there's Dr Penfold, who wants to save his skin and his lucrative practices, the legal and the criminal, a man who, guesses Elverton with a faint tremor of excitement, holds soul and society in equal contempt.

'Bereavement', the woman on the stage enunciates, lifting a white stricken face to the audience, 'is a loss that God, in his Infinite Majesty, may turn to our good, if only – '

In essence, Elverton thinks, his eyes still fixed unwavering on the stage, though ostensibly serving the Crown, he is in a position more or less to determine the outcome of the case according to his own preference. And what's that? Audley Jones's money and influence are worth having. Penfold has marginally less to offer, but he likes Penfold, and liking is a rare enough sensation not to be ignored. After all, Audley Jones and Penfold might be satisfied by the same strategy, leaving Garvey somewhat, but not completely or permanently, disappointed. Audley Jones says his wife might be difficult; says she swears she'll gladly go to prison. Elverton's lip curls; he remembers her initial embarrassment, then her pride and the slight darkening of the thin tone of her voice as later, for some inexplicable reason, she found herself able to snub him, contempt playing in the shadows of her face: 'Mr Elverton, I must introduce you . . . ' She'll play her part, Elverton thinks; one way or another, she'll play her part. All he needs is time, for that Garvey: easy as skittles . . . On stage, the woman lies in picturesque death beneath a painted tree. One of the men meekly stands by her, hands behind his back, head bowed. Sad music seeps up from the pit. The lame soldier returns, stands opposite, then shakes the hand of the other man: '. . . has taken its terrible course. Neither of us will forget this day nor the lessons learned.' They exit separately, a circle of light plays on the clustering of draperies and the chalk-white face of the playing-dead woman; then the house is plunged into violet darkness and volleys of applause. Elverton, high in his box, chuckles as he brings his hands soundlessly together a few times, then makes his way downstairs before the rest of the audience have left their seats. Applause can be heard in the street, which shines with drizzle and gaslight. He makes his way north, walking briskly, but breathing shallow: he knows he'll not sleep tonight.

Jeanne Biggs, dressed in her very best, dodges and careers through the morning flock of city clerks, Mrs Audley Jones's letter tucked safe between her blouse and bodice. She has instructions to wait while the solicitor draws up papers transferring the ownership of Onward House, Home for the Reform of Wayward Girls, to Miss Olivia Handley and Miss Eleanor Wise, the mistress and matron there. Then she will carry the deeds and second letter straight to them; after that, she will visit Clara. Everything about her mission confuses her except its urgency.

'He says he wants to sell Onward House.'

'He can't though, can he? You told me it was yours.'

'There's one way, Jeanne, he could; and between him and Dr Roberts and Elverton they'll think of it. They can say I'm mad. Then everything is his. I know it, he'll try; that's what they're sure to do. But I'll beat them to it. Jeanne, if he finds you've gone, he'll dismiss you, but I'll make sure you've money enough . . . '

Jeanne had thought for a moment it did sound a bit like mad-talk, and even now it is difficult to believe. But those eyes, pleading and burning, that whisper like a conscience or devil, couldn't be ignored. She stops in the solicitor's porch to extricate the first envelope. Her sweat has made the hastily written address run.

Her hands cuffed and locked to the bench behind her, Clara's last tiny hope, the most fragile and therefore the most fiercely clung to, is knocked flying from her grip.

'Your husband told our officer here everything. No doubt he didn't want it on his conscience, poor fellow.' Edmonds, his face puffy and blotched, stares at her, his brown eyes flooding hatred, a steady glint more dangerous by far than the maudlin twinkle of too much drink. 'Terrible state he was in,' he says, 'but clear enough and quite determined to get it all off his mind.'

Clara's blood has turned to water and her eyes are bleeding it; with her hands locked behind her, she can't wipe the salt and mucous from her face, and doesn't care. It isn't like the other time.

'Was it Mrs Audley Jones's idea, or yours?'

She could tell the simple truth that it was Mrs Audley Jones's. She could even exaggerate and say that she was forced into it, or she could protect the other woman by saying it was her own (it doesn't occur to Clara to deny the connection). Not quite obeying any of these policies, she says, 'I can't remember.' It half protects, and she doesn't care to think or decide, doesn't care at all. For Edmonds and Garvey, however, her words are confirmation. They exchange glances and sit easier in their chairs.

'Did you once live on the Peckham Road?'

'Are you the Clara Riley who killed her own baby girl?'

She nods. Snot dribbles over her lips; let it, let it.

'Well, you won't get a fancy barrister this time, not on your side anyway, nor any sympathy either,' says Garvey. 'Your lady friend will be too busy looking after her own reputation. This time you'll get your deserts, and resisting arrest and assaulting police officers on top. Look at her, Edmonds, just look at her.'

They rise together, sign the record and motion the clerk to

follow. As their footsteps fade, Clara shouts, 'She made me, she made me, it was her idea.' For a few seconds, she hates Mrs Audley Jones, remembers standing in her cast-off coat, still undecided, remembers how the words shot out of her mouth not seeming her own . . . 'But no, she didn't,' she says aloud.

'*If you don't want to bear a child and your husband won't interfere with nature, then there is another way*': that was what she'd said. It wasn't Mrs Audley Jones, but the pressure of her own desires and fears that said the words for her. And if it had stayed a secret, it would have worked out for the very best.

'*Good heavens, it wouldn't be any woman's first choice. But we are so rarely allowed our first choice, or any choice at all . . . *' Clara's glad no one came back in answer to her shouts.

'*Don't tell anyone, Clara, no one at all.*' But she, Clara Riley, told Michael; and now he's told the Law.

Jeanne's feet ache, her soaked shoes have lost all their shine, and her fur collar's gone into damp spikes and bald patches, but her heart soars like a kite on the up and up. She's done it: deeds signed, sealed, delivered, and locked in a box; and she's done even more than she was asked, for when Miss Handley and Miss Wise read their letter they went hard and solemn: 'We won't let him do it,' they said. 'We'd die first. Tell her, Jeanne, we'll fight for her and for Onward House whatever happens, tell her just that.' Now all that's left to do is to find out if anything's happened to Clara. Jeanne's riding upstairs on the omnibus. 'We'll fight for her, tell her that. We don't care what people say.' She hears those voices again and again as she watches the view and feels the wind in her face, rushing through the wide streets lined with buildings white as teeth and others grimy as neglected tombs and people scurrying like so many roaches on a kitchen floor. Heavens, I'm getting a wicked taste for adventure, she thinks, leaping from the 'bus unassisted.

She asks directions at the fish stall; now she's nearly done her errands, the sight of shrimps and eels and whelks sprigged with bits of parsley, pale pink and vivid green, makes her mouth water, so she perches on one of the stools to have a dish of shrimps already peeled. How the salty reek of them seeks at memories –

'You can taste the sea in 'em, can't you?' says the fish woman, and she really can, salt and searching as the taste of her own blood when she cuts her finger in the kitchen. 'Plenty more where they come from,' the woman observes, laughing, as she walks off briskly, left again and down the narrow length of Stanley Street. The dull and dirty look of it makes her glad to be in service, able to move all day through large rooms with shiny windows and gilt-framed pictures, kitchen generous and toasting hot, all found bed and board. But what will happen when she's old? Will she end up living somewhere as ugly as this? Or worse? How long will her pile of saved gold coins, barely a finger long, last out? Mrs Audley Jones has always said . . . But what if . . . ?

A wasted-looking man shrugs, and lets her in, points at one of the doors at the end of the passage, standing ajar. Jeanne knocks; there's no answer. The man stands at the bottom of the staircase looking at her. She pushes the door and walks in, noticing immediately that the room is very cold and damp. Michael, his bandage dirty and hanging loose, is sitting at the table with a book open in front of him. He's been humming sacred tunes but stops when he sees Jeanne.

'I beg your pardon, are you Mr Riley? I'm looking for Clara, or news of her.'

Michael gestures slowly round the room. 'I don't know where she is,' he says, and his eyes drop back to the book. Jeanne stands a few seconds, then walks quietly to the door at the back and out into the yard. Rain has turned the trampled sheets into heaps of greyish rag, and broken ends of line trail and whip in the wind. There's the sound of water everywhere, dripping from slates and drains and twigs. A woman calls from the next yard: 'Looking for Clara Riley? The police took her in, search me why, fought like a tiger she did. There were rumours about her but I never believed them, quiet as mice the pair of them.'

'Oh. Thank you,' says Jeanne, and the news, compounded

with the awful dripping of the yard, swamps all the day's successes and excitements. The air she breathes has a faint dismal smell of useless misery, a rotting smell that haunts her during the long gas-lit ride home across the river.

For reasons of security and decorum the Admiral escorts Mrs Audley Jones downstairs to the drawing room for her interview with Elverton, her wrist squeezed hard between his forearm and side.

'Our interests in this matter are identical,' he says, taking the steps two at a time, but slowly, so that she almost stumbles and her hand automatically grasps at the arm she's refused to take. 'So have the sense to realise that, and treat the man as your advisor. Otherwise . . . ' There he stops, leaving the threat open.

Husband and wife wait in armchairs opposite each other. Mrs Audley Jones examines the room; already it is not hers. In her mind's eye she shrinks, then empties it, strips it of paper and cornices, bricks up the bay. Even so, she finds it impossible to imagine the physical reality of prison. To comfort and strengthen herself, she thinks of her secret: Onward House, safe in the hands of Olivia and Eleanor, continuing its work. The thought brings life to her face, a sudden appearance of almost sensual pleasure which bewilders the Admiral as he watches her steadily for signs of fear or tears.

Elverton takes her hand and inclines his head. The Admiral leaves the room.

'Mrs Audley Jones, this is a very grave affair. Procuring an abortion is a crime that has always been taken very seriously indeed, and increasingly so as humanity progresses from barbarism to civilisation. Society looks with horror upon a woman prepared to intervene so cruelly and arrogantly with the new life entrusted by God to woman's keeping.'

'I didn't know you were a religious man, Mr Elverton.'

'We live in a Christian country, Mrs Audley Jones, and those, I assure you, are Christian sentiments. Procuring abortion is considered almost a form of murder. Any person concerned with it is tainted. In this instance, it is charged that you suggested it, that you paid for it, that you made all the arrangements, and took the woman there. Had you not done so, the argument will run, the abortion would not have taken place. Have you considered how you will defend yourself?'

'I'm quite sure my husband has told you of my intentions.'

'They are not realistic intentions, Mrs Audley Jones,' he says quietly. 'They are perhaps the result of the kind of disorganised thinking that can result from a sense of hopeless panic on being discovered. A kind of pride, admirable in its way, but miscalculated and unnecessary: discovery is not conviction.'

'You miss the point, Mr Elverton. I am surprised. I've been led to believe you are an expert in discovering motives.'

I must be careful, she thinks, not to tell him anything he can use to weaken me. Once he finds the target, his aim will be perfect.

'Your husband tells me you are something of a suffragist. Have you considered that your cause will be in no way assisted by being linked with such an affair? Whilst you may obtain some dubious publicity for your own views on motherhood and childbearing, you would be sure to harm your other causes by an equal if not a greater amount.'

'When the movement needs your advice, it will consult you.' Her heart pounds.

Elverton stands in the bay, with his back to the window; she moves to the mantelpiece, scooping her fingers through a bowl of dried petals and lavender. So far as she can see, his face is without expression. Light catches the ends of his hair. She is struggling to keep her own features calm, not to move from her position, nor to stop sifting through the pot-pourri, though its smell is like dust and theatres mixed, stale and sickly. Her limbs long for strong, rhythmic movement and her trailing fingers to clench into fists. His words are guesses, spoken in the dark, yet they frighten her; he will test her systematically, not flailing and blundering, but persistently like a blindfolded person crossing and recrossing a room with the aim of finding something hidden. He's getting closer, and if he should say, 'Mrs Audley Jones, an act of blind adherence to principle and misdirected courage is no compensation for years of cowardice and compromise; it is more an act of selfishness than of heroism', then her face might burst its confines, and the clear thoughts in her head might tumble like a pack of cards into incoherence and contradiction. If that happens, I must not let it show, she tells herself. Elverton, as if smelling fear, walks over and stands at the opposite end of the mantelpiece.

'You probably have little idea of the conditions in prison,' he begins.

'You are mistaken,' she lies.

'There is a way out,' he says, her last remark ignored, 'for which you – we – need Dr Penfold's co-operation. This I have already obtained, his interests being similar to yours.'

'I doubt it.'

Again he ignores her. Sensing triumph, she walks to the window and pulls her fingers across the thin grey coating of water droplets that has condensed on the glass. She breathes deep.

'Dr Penfold will say that you, in a state of some anxiety, brought Clara Riley to him because she had begun to haemorrhage while in this house. You chose to visit him because of his considerable reputation as a gynaecologist. When he examined Clara Riley, he realised she was suffering from an attempt to procure her own abortion by means of an instrument and had no choice but to save her life by bringing the business to its sorry conclusion. You, and Dr Penfold, may on this basis plead not guilty to procuring an abortion. Penfold, of course, may have to defend himself on the lesser charge of concealment, but . . . '

'That is quite enough, Mr Elverton.' Up she soars, effortless as a gull on a clifftop wind. She soars free because she doesn't want his escape, not even for a second does it tempt her; and the relief that her weak spot is his blind spot goes deliciously to her head like sparkling wine.

'Dr Penfold is a liar. I intend to stand by my principles, and by Clara. Please don't interrupt me, you've spoken quite enough. If you say a word more of this I shall be obliged to have your own position in this matter investigated; I'm sure it's highly irregular.'

Elverton's pause gives him away; his next words are bluster.

'Mrs Audley Jones, no one . . . ' His tone is patient, condescending, bluff.

'I assume my husband has promised you a substantial sum to undertake this sordid business; I believe he was intending to sell certain of my property to this end. Perhaps I should warn you, Mr Elverton, that this is something he will not be able to do: I have disposed of the property already. You have little chance of a huge reward, Mr Elverton, and as far as I am concerned, none of success. You waste your time.'

Elverton minutely adjusts a photograph of the Admiral's ship hanging above the mantelpiece.

'Do you know that your doctor believes that you may have to be confined for reasons of mental instability?'

'Get out of here!'

'I inform you only to advise – '

'Get out!'

She strides towards him, her face retaining its hard-won calm, even in rage, as she grasps his shoulders and pushes him to the door. Stumbling, he opens it, pauses a second, before shouting:

'Admiral, quickly: the doctor! Your wife needs attention.'

From behind, Mrs Audley Jones pushes at his arm which bars the door, then runs back into the room. Two sets of heavy, running footsteps grow louder. She throws the petal bowl at the central pane of the fanlight. Her aim is perfect. She picks up a brass stallion and throws that too: the crash is as magnificent as a packed hall standing to shout and stamp its praise. It is the last sound she hears before ether brings its sickly eclipse.

.5.

The Admiral stands at the top of the narrow steps leading to the front door of Onward House, and presses the bell until his finger goes white. He feels for the place that special hatred he normally reserves for enemies of the Empire. He can see nothing of the inside of the house as all the windows are hung with white net. A peculiar mechanical clatter is just audible. He waits and then jabs furiously at the bell a second time, just as the door opens. A girl, dressed plainly like a servant but clearly unabashed by the medals and braid on his jacket and looking him straight in the eye as no servant of his would be allowed to do, asks, 'Good morning, sir, who did you wish to see?'

'Whoever runs this place.'

The girl puts her hand to her cheek where a light spray of spittle has landed. An expression of disgust and contempt passes briefly over her face, unnoticed by the Admiral, who is looking over her head, trying to read a framed notice that fuzzes maddeningly the more he tries to bring his eyes to focus on it.

'I'm Admiral Audley Jones, tell 'em that,' he says, blundering into a small, sparsely furnished room. The clattering seems to be coming from a room immediately above him. It ceases briefly, then recommences with what seems like redoubled vigour. Seconds later, two women of medium height, one about thirty, the other ten years older, enter arm in arm.

Their faces are set firm; they, like the girl, are plainly dressed. Neither, he notices, wears a wedding ring.

'I am Eleanor Handley and this is Olivia Wise,' says the younger of the two. 'We are mistress and matron here; we are the proprietors of Onward House. We manage the place between us. What do you want with us?' They knew he would come: their script is ready, and a half-born smile animates Eleanor's mouth as she waits for his reply.

'I have come, madam, to reclaim this property for a more salubrious use.'

'More salubrious!' explodes Olivia. This level of rudeness was not in their script.

'Your opinion of the uses to which this house is put is quite *superfluous*,' says Eleanor. The rippling, solving word soothes Olivia and gently gathers them back together. 'Since you do not own this property, you cannot reclaim it.' They speak, as planned, in turns.

'Onward House used to belong to your wife. You may be unaware of it, but since 1871 Acts have been passed which enable a married woman to own her own property, and to dispose of it.'

'Your wife gave Onward House to us. You can send your solicitor to examine the deeds, if you like. They are all perfectly in order.'

'Deeds indeed, what do women know of property and legal matters? My wife was not in her right mind when she signed those deeds, if she did.'

Olivia does not falter. 'We know enough to know what's ours. Your shouting is disturbing the classes being held upstairs.'

'By what right do a pair of spinsters come between a husband and his wife's affairs? Tell me that.'

'We already have.' Olivia and Eleanor feel they are acquitting themselves well. But how to slip in between his hail of invective and their counter-thrusts of contemptuous politeness: 'Tell us, how is your wife, *where is she?*' How on earth to do that? Admiral Audley Jones, the backs of his legs trembling with rage thinks, old maids, they're all the same, their brains are overworked and their natural functions inhibited so that they've forgotten how a lady should behave. The world would be a better place without women. There are not enough men in this country, that's why it's losing its grip.

'The whole of Eve's daughters' nest of vipers deserve to be locked away, the whole blasted tribe of you. You'll hear from me again, you can depend on it,' he shouts as he pushes past them to the door, his eyes wide, but focused above their heads.

'Locked away': he has more or less answered their question. Upstairs, twenty typewriters, fallen silent during the climax of the argument, begin their rattling and ringing again. Some of the young women in Onward House hope to work in offices or publishing companies; others remember the lecture given by a kind-faced lady from the Female Emigration Society and hope to type amidst the crystal white wastes of Canada, or in the tropical-bird-thronged suburbs of the more civilised parts of Australia. Typing's clean and constant rhythm, the very newest thing, opens doors on dreams, albeit tidy-minded ones. There are other girls, however, whose fingers, nimble enough at any other task, crash and stumble over the neat-ranked keys, whose minds wander on wild unorchestrated fantasies as words creep and blurt mis-shapen and mis-spelled across the foolscap sheet. They type only because it is a pre-condition of residence in Onward House. The girl who answered the door to the Admiral, Alice Toms, is one of these. When Olivia and Eleanor do not return to the classroom, even though the Admiral has gone, banging the door behind him, Alice takes the opportunity to abandon her machine mid-word and go downstairs. Olivia and Eleanor are sitting together on the sofa, their usual stiffness gone out of them, looking to Alice just like any ordinary pair of women.

'Is there anything I can do?' asks Alice, shocked by their unguardedness, by the signs of confusion and worry on their faces.

'I don't know, Alice, I don't think so,' says Eleanor. Alice is frightened: despite the daily torture of typing, she has grown to love Onward House, to depend on the attention duly paid to her, the hours for reading and sitting quiet on her own, the meals, the company –

'That Admiral can't take Onward House away, can he?' she asks.

Olivia and Eleanor's eyes meet, dull, uncertain. Suddenly Olivia breaks free.

'No,' she says to Alice and Eleanor. 'We are going to turn Onward House into a proper charitable trust that belongs to no one. He may try, but he won't succeed.'

Peacehaven was originally built as a gentlemen's residence; the upper stories have been altered and their windows barred, but the downstairs rooms are unchanged. Generous bays offer views of a geometric garden, its regular lines disrupted by faults in the glass; beyond it, a wall. The country they drove through was flat as a plate, a mere baseline of land for huge displays of turbulent sky and a track for hungering winds that seem to bear in from all sides at once. Even through the thick-built walls of Peacehaven these winds can be felt, not whistling but battering and straining like wrestlers never tired.

'I thought you might give the second opinion, old fellow,' Dr Roberts says to Dr Ampleforth. 'I'd have been inclined simply to diagnose a morbid melancholia but for the attack I described, which makes it so much more complex and serious. More alarming, and completely without cause. The man was the family lawyer. Thank goodness he's not taking any action, but you can imagine how the Admiral feels. Duty calling him away so much of the time, he would, of course, be prepared to pay for the very best treatment and accommodation.'

'Of course, of course,' replies Ampleforth with every appearance of genuine sympathy. 'This sort of tragedy is surprisingly common; most of our patients here are ladies of a certain age. Women were created to bear children, or, if you like, "evolved" so to do, and when this is no longer possible, their grip on reason is seldom unimpaired.'

The two men nod in brief and casual agreement as at a well-known truth reiterated for reassurance. The weather's better down south. Brown eggs are better than white.

'Well,' says Ampleforth eventually, 'we shall see what is the matter.' He walks over to Mrs Audley Jones.

I'll say nothing to him, she promises herself, since nothing I say will get me out of here. Say nothing, and do nothing, perhaps in time I will forget where I am . . . But the doctor hasn't come to speak. He begins to feel her skull through her hair, systematically pressing its hollows and tracing its bumps. A huge involuntary shudder jerks Mrs Audley Jones half out of her seat.

'Now . . . ' He presses her back down, but does not continue his examination.

'I know there are new theories and techniques,' he addresses Roberts, 'some of which are available here – for in desperate cases who would not try any cure, however far-fetched? But I strongly believe that the physical and the mental are one and the same, and though we cannot see the mind itself, the body is here before us – '

'Quite,' says Roberts in agreement. '*Mens sana in corpore sano.*'

Oh my God, thinks Mrs Audley Jones, staring resolutely at the quavering lines of the garden's beds, borders and paths: this is the underside of the bright ordinary world, the very image of hell. In the intensity of her awareness of the invisible constrictions the two doctors, hell's genuine dressmakers, are so expertly, so casually tightening to a perfect fit around her, she forgets the world was never really bright and beautiful, nor sleep ever as regular as clockwork and sweet as balm. Ampleforth signs. Roberts' and the Admiral's names are already on the papers. They laugh and light pipes like men who've sold a stack of shares or a herd of sheep.

' – rest of her things can be sent for – '

' – not necessary, my dear friend, not necessary at all . . .'

Mrs Audley Jones's mind is space, shocked empty; and thoughts, brief and senseless as moths, flutter through, lost, disconnected. I should have done more. I was too timid.

119

'. . . another war so soon! There's already a shortage of men . . . but it's unlikely, don't you think?'

How do I keep sane in a madhouse? Is it worth trying?

'All liberals are the same – '

'And how the speed of change accelerates: in ten years, twenty, who knows what science and engineering will have brought to civilisation? I'll ring for Matron, and the orderly.'

Perhaps someone will get me out? Perhaps even now, Eleanor and Olivia . . . Dreams of rescue: that way real madness lies.

Matron and the orderly stand on either side of her chair. 'Come along, Mrs Audley Jones, stand up, please.'

'You're in the best of hands, my dear,' says Dr Roberts from across the room; the man who prescribed her powders for headaches, delivered her son, and took out her womb using the most modern anaesthetic techniques, now confining her to Peacehaven, Private Residence for The Insane. He interrupts his tête-à-tête with his one-time pupil, Dr Ampleforth, now a specialist in diseases of the mind, to bid her good-bye. 'I shall visit, depend on it,' he says.

'Stand up, please.' The voice's threat of touch is enough; she stands. I'm a coward through and through. What then? Living in silence, or shouting to the grave? She chooses silence, that hangs poised on gimbals in the eye of the storm, the swishing and churning and slops of memory and thought.

The court is packed, damp and hot, for spring is beginning with daily pyrotechnics of brilliant sunshine, sudden dark and lightning-rent downfalls that flood gutters and cause accidents. One of the women killed her baby before, but got off, the other one's an Admiral's wife. No one can quite remember whether it was a baby boy or baby girl she killed. Some have come for the sickly-sweet inside lurch such stories bring, others simply because Counsel for the Prosecution is William Elverton, the Alchemist of the Bar, said to be worth hearing whatever case he takes.

Abortion. 'A primitive and bestial crime no longer to be tolerated in a nation that cherishes its children,' says the *London Gazette.* 'No woman worthy of the name . . . ' Clara thinks: it's not like the other time, everything's changed. There's no one to talk to her about how an unjust law can always be bent, there's no one to talk to at all, except the police and the warders, and she can feel their hate like an invisible whip playing about her. What's going to happen to me? What can they do to me? Will they hang me? she asks; but then she answers, no, it'll be all right, it'll be just like last time and everyone will understand in the end. She's seen no windows for weeks now, and the thought of never throwing one open again is too much like death to bear thinking on.

It's not like the other time. New advertisement hoardings bear pictures of soft-faced blue and pink fluffy cosseted babies asleep or sipping broth or cured of colic, babies sleeping safe in special cots and infant beds with their hair brushed to a flaxen shine, tucked and ruched and reclining beatific in maternal arms. The world's their oyster, at the price of *Encyclopedia Britannica*; they lie like Buddhas awaiting offerings of patent infant vests and teething rusks: keep the windows open, nothing surpasses mother's milk, as good for the temper as it is for the bones. Children seem scarcer and more precious than in the old Queen's days; perhaps that is why so many smile their innocent but compelling smiles from billboards and newspaper pages.

Miss Handley and Miss Wise are in the public gallery. They've written three times to Peacehaven and been told that Mrs Audley Jones is performing light tasks and that idleness is one of the greatest causes of derangement in women; they almost laughed, for they never knew anyone who worked as hard as Christine Audley Jones. All the letters concluded: 'the patient is, however, severely disturbed and no visitors are allowed without her husband's permission.' They've been to Scotland Yard and been told to mind their own business; they've been to the Women's League, and then they saw it in the papers, hired a temporary mistress and came, bringing

Alice Toms who wept until they let her. Now they're glad of her because she's been in courts before and can tell them how it goes.

The press gallery is full; the case is expected to last, and is remarkable in that three people, two of them respectable and wealthy, the third notorious, have been charged with the abortion of the same foetus.

Since the 1861 Offences Against the Person Act, says the Gazette, *it has been an offence for a woman to abort or attempt to abort herself, an offence equal in gravity and severity of punishment to that of a person attempting to bring about an abortion on a pregnant woman, with or without her consent. It is then surely arguable that on any occasion when a woman seeks abortion at the hands of another, or others, all parties are equally guilty. It is to be hoped that the prosecution, and the enforcers of our law, will in this case be bold enough to establish this clearly in the courts. This would surely be a well-directed attempt to stamp out this growing horror in our midst. For if such women know that they are not exempt from the arm of justice then they will be less inclined to seek the illegal operation; since immoral practitioners ply their despicable trade only because there are women actively seeking their services; it is to be hoped that the result of setting a noteworthy precedent for prosecuting the mother (who is, after all, ultimately responsible for the whole sordid business) would be, over the years, an end to the murder of unborn infants.*

The Gazette reporter is an acquaintance of Elverton's, and indeed his report contains the substance of a suggestion Elverton offered to Inspector Garvey, inch by inch and seeming not to care, to the end of convincing him it would be wise to charge Dr Penfold only with failing to report the abortion. Convicting Mrs Audley Jones would itself have been something worthwhile, seeing as ladies of the upper classes so rarely met with justice, he said, but that's no longer possible. Prosecuting Penfold alone is scarcely worth the trouble. On the other hand, he continued, I've had another idea . . . Making history, Garvey repeats to himself, tentative yet admiring like a man seeing himself in a pricey suit; the judicial system needs pushing from those who work at its rough end. 'It's a risk,' said Elverton, 'but I'll take it on if you wish, you know I don't like tame cases.'

'We make a fine partnership,' said Garvey, and both men glanced over their shoulders. They weren't meant to have that kind of conversation. 'After all,' said Garvey, 'those whores ought to be punished, it's them as asks for it and sets the whole thing off.'

The public gallery seems to be occupied mainly by members of the gentler sex, fascinated perhaps by the aberration of nature's ways to be brought before them. Recent events have shown that the suffragettes also hold life less dear than do their more womanly sisters, and indeed, several women noted for the extremity of their opinions are in the public gallery. One can only guess at their reasons for absenting themselves from speechifying, bomb-making and brick throwing, to watch this trial. Rumour has it that Mrs Audley Jones herself was active in the suffrage movement. This cannot but be significant. The press have been unable to contact Admiral Audley Jones or his wife since the news broke, and indeed their house in Penley Square appears to have been closed.

The second accused woman, tried some years ago for the murder of her five-day-old baby girl but, in the judge's wisdom (which will doubtless not go unchallenged this week), absolved from punishment on the grounds of temporary postpartum derangement, is said to be unrepresented. If this case ends in conviction, with such an upstanding judge as Mr Justice Brinley sitting, the full penalty of the law as it stands can be expected to fall on all three defendants. Cases like this show only too clearly that a certain inclination to leniency which has prevailed in the past in respect of those few women who came before the courts for crimes of violence or immorality is an error, for such chivalry undermines the deterrent effect of the law . . .

Clara wonders what Mrs Audley Jones will say. She tells herself again and again that she's not alone. She can't believe they'll send a lady down, an Admiral's wife. Oh yes, Mrs Audley Jones will have it all worked out. It was her that suggested it, it wasn't Clara's fault, it wasn't even wrong. Edmonds and Garvey tried to frighten her that it was murder, but it wasn't, it wasn't. She can hardly even remember it now: the pain burned it from her memory, minute by minute as it happened, but she knows she was lying down with something in her mouth, wanting to scream; she wasn't murdering anyone. She can remember stifling the little girl. Garvey and Edmonds know about that too. They told her there's no difference, but she can remember that awful tightening, like she was a steel hawser, accidently unfastened, with the ship straining out to sea, and then she broke and she was the ship instead, steaming out into a painted picture sea. They said it was madness, but it's madness she can remember clear as if it was everyday real. She can remember that sudden heightening of silence that meant a life had drained away – oh no, it wasn't the same at all. Garvey'd come in, stiff collar sticking into his neck, eyes burning out of a face limp with hatred.

'I've news for you,' he'd said, 'we're treating this case as what it is, murder, that's what, and if I had my way you'd swing for it, all of you.' And Edmonds, giving her the fist-and-cock smile of a man late home on pay-day night, he'd said,

'P'raps she'd like to see a priest, eh?'

So what she did to the girl was real, was madness, was murder but they called it something different, yes, because some killing's worse than others and the reasons ought to count. But the reasons are the same, she thinks, surely what I did the second time's not as bad as the girl, but why is everything so much worse?

'It's interesting,' says Elverton to Garvey as they wait in the lobby, 'that in that other case I handled for you recently, the key to it was in discovering a motive. Here, an important factor will be the absence of one. The woman has no children. It's not as if she was pressed beyond endurance, the jury's unlikely to shed too many philanthropic tears.'

*

Dressed with the utmost sobriety, Dr Penfold waits alone, winding and resetting his watch.

Acting on information, that's what they'd promised to say. The case stood on its own, and he wouldn't have to stand in court and swear, nor look Clara in the face. He needn't have come at all. Michael hates the Admiral's wife. She encouraged Clara to want more than she was meant to have, she gave her that coat, fed her with dainty sandwiches and cake so as she'd always want it: it was her fault for tempting. And that Admiral's wife was after votes for women and it was one of those that threw the brick that sent glass into that girl's face. He hates Mrs Audley Jones, he's come to see her in the dock . . . and Clara, he might glimpse her from behind, in the dock as well, his wife that grew so tender but never sung a lullaby, that nursed him but never nursed a child. A devil beneath, he mutters to himself, the Devil has many guises. And a blind eye often weeps.

Initially the case is held back while documents and medical witnesses are presented in an application to have Mrs Audley Jones exempted from the proceedings.

In view of the fact that she has recently been confined to an insane asylum, with little prospect of recovery in the immediate future, the application was granted. There will be those with curious minds who will ask whether the lady in question has not preferred the comfort of rural exile to the shame of prison bars; but those of a kinder disposition will perhaps conclude that the raucous rantings of her suffragist friends have distressed and finally deranged a delicate constitution, and that Mrs Audley Jones, caught up in this sorry business, is to be pitied rather than blamed.

Mr William Elverton appears unperturbed where many men would be dismayed at the difficulties which one might surmise, the absence of one of the accused might create in presenting a coherent

125

account of a crime for which three people are simultaneously on trial. This sang-froid is not altogether surprising as Mr Elverton has a reputation for rising to any occasion, as well as one for success. Indeed, his largely silent presence today in court was extremely impressive, his physique is almost ill-developed, and yet there is about him an air of immense strength of character, of a relentless-ness of intellect and singleness of purpose such as are possessed by very few, and which must have their source in the moral heart of the man.

Mr William Elverton's arteries and veins are empty, blood pounds only in his temples and the innermost cavities of his ears. His intense excitement is mingled with fear and exactly matched by a self-control which prevents any visible expression of his mood. But beneath the gracefully gathered folds of his gown, each one of his muscles pulls to its utmost and is counterbalanced by the pull of its opposite, so that he stands locked and each movement feels like an abrupt and temporary escape from paralysis. His penis erect, even his toes are stiff, but the voice that issues from his bolted body is smooth and splendid, unhesitating and modulated as solemn music. He will be calling Edmonds, Dr Penfold, Dr Roberts and Admiral Audley Jones, and he knows they will play their parts. He must also call Clara Riley, and she is an unknown quantity. The jury look unremarkable. He decides to call Penfold first, and then Clara Riley. He meets Garvey's eye momentarily, a soft dog's eye stupidly waiting to make history, blissfully unaware quite how audacious Elverton is being. Mrs Audley Jones is safe in Peacehaven, but the Admiral wants her name, which is his, to be cleared. 'At any price,' he's reiterated daily, 'if you can do it, you can name your price, and count on me in the future.' For a brief instant Elverton, even as he stands waiting to open his case, amuses himself by imagining the Admiral's disappointment and rage were he to betray him at the last moment by arguing Riley and Audley Jones in conspiracy, Penfold guilty only of concealment. Cat among the pigeons. But no, this is neither the time nor the place.

This is the easy part, Elverton reminds himself, as sweat

breaks out beneath his wig and on his back and legs; the most important work is already done: the persuasion, the financial arrangements, the records. This is just the public show.

Michael does gardens in Hampstead, and he's losing pay and probably the job by coming today. He watches the back of her head, her hair still dark with almost a wave in it, until his good eye goes blurred. She's not yet spoken a word or turned her head at all, but he'll keep coming till it's over. He sits stiff and hungry between a lady in grey silk and a governessy-looking girl. He's dressed in his Sunday best, shaved close, his fingernails scraped till you'd never know he was a working man, but the lady beside him still can't bear it if her glance wanders and catches the puckered lid of the scarred eye that shows it doesn't see.

Clara doesn't look at William Elverton, but stares instead at her hands, swollen from inaction but smooth now, almost as smooth as Mrs Audley Jones's. Elverton is stating the case against her, but Clara can't attend, stands in hollow shocked loneliness: Mrs Audley Jones is not coming to court, she's been confined insane. It's a betrayal. Insanity, Clara knows, saves you from the law, it saved her once, and so she does not believe that Mrs Audley Jones is mad, nor that she'll never be cured; no, she thinks she's clever, and she hates her, screams silently at being left alone. And what is she going to say, all alone, when the questions begin? She steals a glance at Dr Penfold, the man who pulled her insides out and pressed his hand over her mouth to stop her crying out loud and called her a *class of person*, and she hates him too, hates him from the bottom of her guts. She hates Michael too, he's got her to this and now he'll be telling himself it's God's punishment. She hates him for his humility, for the stupidity that has made him cruel, for his cowardice, the cowardice of sitting in their room silent and refusing food; waiting he must've been for that little army to come and take his wife away, praying in his head, where was the good in that? Thinking of her betrayal whets

127

her hate's edge until it severs the air around her so that she's utterly separate, completely parted from all she knows of people. That death's head of a man is going to ask her questions, she doesn't know what, and she's going to have to defend herself.

Clara Riley was charged with attempting to abort herself and with procuring an abortion for herself. Charges of assaulting police officers and resisting arrest are to be heard separately. Doctor Penfold was charged only with concealing an abortion. There were no charges against Mrs Audley Jones who has been exempted from trial. Dr Penfold pleaded guilty, and Clara Riley, after noticeable hesitation, not guilty.

Mr Elverton set out the case for the prosecution cogently and, at some points, one might opine, almost too graphically. He began, as is customary: 'Gentlemen of the Jury –' and immediately there was an outburst from the public gallery. 'Gentlemen! Things'd be a sight different if there was ladies on the jury as well', and a young woman was removed from the gallery. This is not the place to deplore at length the unseemly behaviour of the suffragettes nor indeed is it necessary, since such behaviour condemns itself. Mr Elverton continued: 'Standing before you is Clara Riley, a woman of forty-two, married for eighteen years to a carpenter's labourer, living in modest but decent accommodation and circumstances, and employed most of her life as a wash woman. An ideal couple of their class, but childless, a fact which makes the events of the third of November nineteen hundred and nine even more repugnant. On this date Clara Riley arrived at the home of Mrs Audley Jones to collect her washing work, rather later than usual and appearing unwell. She was indeed suffering as the result of an attempt to abort herself by means of an instrument . . . When . . . bleeding . . . became apparent, the lady of the house, in some distress and herself unwell, took Clara Riley to Dr Penfold, a surgeon with some reputation in matters of female health. Dr Penfold, who has pleaded guilty to concealment of an abortion, had little choice but to . . . and bring the business to its sorry close. Mrs Audley Jones naturally paid Dr Penfold for his services, and Clara Riley once more had prevented her offspring from enjoying the life God gave it.

'I say once more, for it is material to this case, and should not be forgotten, that in 1888 Clara Riley was acquitted of the murder of her five day-old baby on the grounds of postpartum insanity. That baby was killed by stifling. Clara Riley may be a respectable member of the working class and may live decently and comfortably, but she is a woman prepared to go to any lengths, and to break the law and the ten commandments from which it derives, in order to avoid the natural duty of motherhood . . . '

Miss Handley sits alone in the typing room of sleepbound Onward House, composing a letter to the *Suffrage Gazette*. She has been near to tears all day. Alice Toms has been cautioned and barred from reattending the court. Not only is Mrs Audley Jones shut away unreachable, under false pretences, but what stretches the insides of her throat and baffles her fingers so that she, an exceptionally rapid touch-typist, has to look at the keys, is the memory of Clara Riley's distant face, a sea of panic and incomprehension, with her two dark eyes beached like wrecks in the aftermath of a storm that's washed all life away.

'. . . a disgusting spectacle', she writes, 'of British injustice, for Mrs Riley, an ordinary working woman, is to be pitted against the cleverest barrister in the country, unrepresented and with no advice as to points of law or procedure. In a case where a rare and vindictive interpretation of the law is being assumed, this is unforgivable. Mr Elverton's opening speech appeared to break all the rules of evidence, as well as those of fair play, and yet no one objected . . . The Riley case, where a woman is being tried for expelling the contents of her womb, rather than risk repeating the temporary insanity which once drove her to infanticide, is a terrible example of the inferior status women have in law . . . There is a dreadful hypocrisy in all this, for sadly there must be thousands of abortions each year, and yet how often are cases brought to court, let alone cases like this, where not only the doctor but the woman herself is to be prosecuted. Clara Riley is a scapegoat. Even if the premises for the prosecution are accepted, it appears she is now standing trial alone for a crime that involved several people. Many things in this trial give grounds for suspicion. Much moralising is done nowadays about motherhood, but surely an unwilling mother . . .'

Miss Handley feels her letter growing incoherent. There are so many things to be said, and besides she herself once went to Birmingham to get an abortion from a woman there said to be safe and cheap, and of course she wished it hadn't happened, none of it, but she prides herself on the work she's done since and that she'd never have done without it. Oh what would have happened to me, she thinks, and turns back to her paper to avoid the thought.

'. . . Until women are enfranchised and allowed to sit on juries, and until laws that are just have been made, such examples of monumental injustice will recur . . .'

It's going to take so long, she thinks, staring at the shameful page. Many of her sisters in the movement will condemn what Christine Audley Jones has done as inopportune or immoral, and they will condemn what she has written. It's going to take so very long.

Clara says nothing about what she thinks of God, and swears the oath in a small voice like that of a child's trying not to annoy. She can't feel her feet, and there's no grip at all in her hands. They've all lied. She never tried to do it herself, she wasn't bleeding when she got there, and Mrs Audley Jones, oh how could she? How could she? But Dr Penfold's stood up, and said yes, that's what he did, he's very sorry, but in the circumstances . . . they've worked it all out.

'Would you like to address the court, Mrs Riley?' asks the judge. Clara shakes her head. Young William Elverton stands to question her. William, she thinks, William, that's what I'd have called the first, the one I left in Clapham. She looks Elverton in the face and thinks it could be him, the one I left, Marcus Rosenbury's bastard. Why, oh why? It wasn't my fault.

But William was only a secret, half-name, no one knew. So it isn't him. Yet he's got the same lips, the same metal-grey eyes. If it's him they know about that as well; no one's said, but that's what I'm here for as well.

'Are you Mrs Clara Riley?' he asks and then her answer's drowned in a rumble of shouts from the gallery.

'Baby killer!'

'Unnatural!'

'Massacring the innocent!'

'Little children, little children!'

And someone calls for silence, but no one stops the shouting; it swells and swells and seems to fill the whole high room.

'Vermin!'

'She-devil! Case for the rope.'

'Little children, little children.'

Stunned, Clara turns to face the crowds she'd not realised were there, a writhing gallery of faces, cracked and mobilised by the excitement of hate and the sounds of their own shouting voices, usually modulated and dull, now filled out and amplified in the domed space so they can hear in their own tones the moral authority of God or King.

'Baby killer!'

Something hurtles through the air and spatters Clara's face with cold juice as it hits the witness box railings. Ushers begin to clear the gallery as Clara, her legs soft and unsteady as those of something newborn, or something nearly dead, is taken back to her cell.

The moral outrage of the crowd, unintentionally stirred by Mr Elverton's address to the court and perhaps irritated by the brazen and unconcerned manner of Mrs Riley, a broad-shouldered, rather muscular woman who stood with her head high and her large hands resting on the rail, broke the bounds of normal restraint, but then this is not a normal case. The incident was, of course, regrettable, yet at the same time a testimony to the depths of public outrage.

*

The crowd, cowed by threats and now ashamed of its raucousness, waits in line for readmission. Miss Handley and Miss Wise are at the very end of the queue, arm in arm, and silent. Michael stands in front of the woman who won't look at his eye and listens as she talks in a breathy whisper to an elderly man.

'Such a very unnatural act,' her small gloved hand tightens on his arm, 'unimaginable. When I think of my own little angels at play in the park or sleeping in the nursery, my heart just shudders at the thought . . .'

'Inconceivable, inconceivable. You must keep calm. But you know, my dear, there are people whose sensitivities are scarcely developed, whose souls are so brutish as to be untouched by even the most elementary of human emotions . . .'

'There's reasons why people do terrible things,' Michael interrupts angrily.

The blunt sound of his voice, as much as the words and feelings he flounders in, shocks him. He's spoken to no one for days and the sound is like a ghost or a stranger; and as he speaks he remembers for a few moments, body and soul the instant just before Clara began telling him, when they were both overcome by their own tenderness and time and memories, so that nothing, not the everlasting damp nor work nor blindness nor a thousand disappointments, existed; and in that beautiful limbo they'd spun around themselves a cocoon of all the most soothing and generous emotions. For a terrifying second Michael finds himself almost understanding why Clara so wanted to be free. He's prey to a sinful wish that she'd never told him her secret, then he could have floated the rest of his days with Clara in ignorant bliss. Suppose he did wrong reporting her? He shakes his head to chase the thought away. A sin is a sin and a selfish desire is to be overcome. They file back into the gallery to await the court's return. No one sits next to Michael, whose lips have begun to move with silent, useless prayers.

'Mrs Riley, have you had any children?' Elverton asks conversationally. Clara, her hands pressed to her sides to keep them still, nods.

'Please answer so that the court can hear.'

'Yes, I have,' she says, and knows that next he'll ask her how many, and she'll have to lie; she's got to say one not two, unless the termination counts; they already know about the little girl. But is it a trick? Perhaps they do know about the one she left as well? William, William, he must be the one, come after all these years, just like his father, to force and push and punish her, just the same. Pursuing you like devils forever after. Was it Michael she'd seen when she looked up at the gallery, his loose lips moving with the shouts, 'She-devil, she-devil', or was it imagination, a one-eyed ghost come to torment her? And next he'll ask what happened to it, or them, and lies or truth it won't matter, the crowd will shout just the same and they won't care about the details. She did do it, but she's pleaded not guilty: no one'll understand that. William will catch her out, good and proper, just like his father did. It didn't happen how they said, but they've sworn the same oath as me. It must've been a mistake they let me off before. I can't answer these questions, none of them, they don't fit –

Elverton is looking down at his notes to choose his next question. He reads, how many now living and dead? Have you always wanted to be childless? He feels inexplicably uneasy, almost nauseous, without knowing why. He clears his throat and looks up. 'How –'

'Can I change what I said?' Clara asks. 'I want to change it to guilty, I did it so I must be guilty.'

The journalists attribute Clara Riley's court-room confession to the extraordinary presence of Mr William Elverton and his interrogatory skill, described by the *London Gazette* as 'an almost clairvoyant moral intensity and perspicacity'. They dwell at length on the pause before his question and the stern look that followed it, deemed to have cowed Clara Riley into admitting her guilt, like a look into the eyes of the Almighty. Elverton's reputation is to be solidified and burnished; he has reached the position of respect of which he has always dreamed.

'My Lord, I have nothing more to add,' he says to the judge, and sits down abruptly *as if* writes the *Record, after some intense effort of spiritual concentration.*

'Do you wish to say anything to the court before sentence is passed?' the judge asks. Although his voice is clear, he seems very far away and his features have melted into a pale blur, and when Clara turns to look at the gallery that, too, is a sea of white patches, and the hissing in her ears might be the crashing of those waves she's never heard; but up there in the gallery they're silent, willing her to either silence or speech, but which she can't tell, and will the shouting start again? Clara sways to the rhythm of the sea in her ears.

'Say something; tell them why, or they'll slaughter you!' shrieks a voice from the gallery, a woman's voice splintering under the impact of its own audacity, then bundled into silence. Clara steadies herself on the smooth balustrade of the dock.

'I just didn't want children,' she says. 'I wanted to be comfortable and sit down at night – I can't bear screaming on and on – I like my peace and I knew I couldn't love a child and so I never wanted to have one. And I didn't know how not to have one and my husband, because of being a religious man, would never . . .'

Michael stands up and leans forward, straining to catch her words. No one can make out what she's saying, for the court's echoes, which William Elverton can use to such effect, wash her thin quiet voice to a meaningless rasp.

'Speak up, Mrs Riley,' says the judge, but Clara wants only for it to be done with, and she shakes her head in silence.

'Mrs Riley, you have been found guilty of attempting to procure an abortion, and of procuring an abortion. You are a woman who has repeatedly and deliberately flown in the face of the values of our civilisation and of the laws that protect those values, and you have involved other people in your attempt to do so, without care for their reputation or moral well-being. For your own good, as much as for the purposes of punishment, I am treating a grave offence seriously. However, there are so few modern precedents for this case that I have had to consider the sentence with the utmost care, and have decided that you shall be sentenced to remain in prison at His Majesty's Pleasure, that is, until such time as it may (or may not) be deemed that you are no longer a danger to society . . .'

With his eyes closed, Michael listens to the judge's voice, time-laden and oh, so sure, and he feels the words and the steady cadence of their sentences dissolve his doubts and turn loss to emptiness, filling him with the dark heavy wine of tragedy and conclusion. He finds he is able to pray again to the God whose suffering and goodness is beyond all things human, who, knowing all, apportions and judges, tests, tries and delivers finally, as now, finally, what is right without end must be. Oh Lord, I submit and do not presume, it must be, it is good, thy will be done forever, amen.

An inspired sentence, writes the *Daily Chronicle*, in which justice is tempered with the possibility of mercy.

Liars and hypocrites, thinks Clara. Him and the Pope and the rest of them won't let you have a life. I killed my baby girl. I had a termination. I didn't want it, none of it. It may be all wrong, all wrong what I did, but I didn't want none of it, and it needn't have been. Marcus Rosenbury set me up good and proper, and then the Pope and this bastard William Elverton, they've set me up and now they'll lock me up. His Majesty's Pleasure. Why can't they let you have your living and leave you be, the fight's gone out of me. You might as well be in prison.

Clara lets them take her away.

'It's not as if she'd have any more children at her age,' Eleanor whispers to Olivia. 'It's a life sentence in disguise.'

'He's hedging his bets in case there's a fuss. But I don't think there will be, not enough to make a difference, not now.' Olivia sounds tired and dull.

'You mean she'll just stay in there until she dies – ' Eleanor is close to tears, her voice breaking gruffly out of its whisper.

'I hope not. We won't forget, will we? Not her nor Christine. We'll do all we can – ' Olivia says to comfort, but thinks as she speaks how little they have so far been able to do for Christine Audley Jones, how little power they have in the world. She wonders what Clara Riley might think of the pair of them, standing there free and helpless.

'Some people, women as well as men, make very harsh judgements. Call for social purity and adherence to duty. I've said such things myself . . .'

'She must think Christine's betrayed her.'

'I don't know what to do about that letter from the Admiral, Eleanor.'

'Nothing. Tear it up. Let him waste his time. We're not going to let this stand. We're going to do more than remember, we're going to fight.'

'What else,' says Eleanor, allowing herself to lean heavily on Olivia's offered arm.

Elverton sits with the Admiral in the drawing room of number five Penley Square. The house is very quiet. Jeanne and the kitchen maid have both handed in their notice.

Elverton's account is now fat from the proceeds of the Admiral's shares in guns and African mines, Penfold's ill-gotten gains, Garvey's usual 'token of esteem' and his official fee as well.

'There is another matter I would like you to undertake for me,' the Admiral says, sure of his man, yet at the same time deeply embarrassed. He embarks on his second glass of wine. 'Seeing how magnificently you dealt with the other sorry business. It's a matter of some property which my wife, just prior to her confinement in Peacehaven, signed over to a pair of half-crazy spinsters. Quite a large property, at present being

136

used as some kind of school for women picked up from the streets. I want it back, of course – '

'I believe you mentioned it to me once before,' Elverton says coldly. 'I advised you not to pursue it, so far as I remember.'

The Admiral takes another drink, noisily. 'I wrote to them and they didn't answer, they had the audacity not to reply,' he says.

'It's not the kind of work that I do. It would not interest me, I'm afraid. I have no desire to be seen standing up in court with the aim of destroying a charitable concern. Besides, it would take a very long time and the outcome would be far from certain.'

'It's a simple matter of reclaiming property which my wife was not in a fit state to give. Do you understand what I'm saying?'

'Yes, but I beg to differ. It is not simple legally, not in any other way. The grounds for your wife's confinement, whilst necessary and obvious to yourself and those of us concerned in the matter, may perplex some people. Your part in it may not, perhaps, meet with universal approval . . . A legal case is a very complicated thing, Admiral, demanding as I said before immense strategic skill, a sophisticated understanding of politics, emotion and the treacherous shifts of public concern. It has to be planned and controlled in these respects as much as in purely legal terms.'

Elverton feels slightly hollow as he speaks, painfully conscious that what had happened to Clara Riley in the pause between one question and the next had taken him entirely by surprise, and that the accidentally fortuitous could just as easily be disastrous.

'Divorce, for instance, is a legal possibility, but often a social handicap.'

'I am not interested in people's opinions of my actions, I want that house. Will you undertake it?'

'No.'

The Admiral puts his empty glass heavily on the table and

137

rings for someone to show Elverton out. 'I thought you were a man of principle,' he says.

'So do other people, and I would not have them think otherwise.'

No one answers the bell.

'This country's full of young men with too much education and insufficient manhood. There's neither honour nor discipline. That's why the women are giving trouble.' Rather than ring again, the Admiral shows Elverton out himself.

.6.

The first touch of icy water curdles Clara's flesh. The prison bathouse is the coldest place she's ever been. The only steam is that on her and the warden's breath. Her skin puckers, turns purple, white and blue. The latherless carbolic soap slips time and time again between her fingers. The warden stands close by the bath, her stare unwavering. Humiliation and the intense cold paralyse her body and mind alike. Numb, she's bundled to medical examination in a grey towel stiff with crusts of soap, waiting in line. They look down there to see if you've got the pox. What're you in for? What's the matter with you, cat got your tongue? Too good for the likes of us are you? Say something or they'll slaughter you, the broken voice from the court-room echoes in her head. 'Abortion,' she says, 'abortion.'

'It seems you're expecting, Riley.'

'No I'm not,' Clara says. Surprise makes her forthright, she looks straight up. The eyes she meets know they are right and flicker with impatience.

'Well you certainly aren't the Virgin Mary. When was your last monthly period? Hurry up – '

'No I can't be,' Clara says. The words sound very muffled and distant in her ears; everything in the room seems to be tilting away from her and she wants to sit down. Are they trying to torture her into madness?

139

'Listen, Riley, I'm a woman of the world, there's no point in pretending. If it isn't your husband's I don't really care. And don't waste your time acting ashamed, you can't sink much lower than this here, can you? Whoever it is, they'll be after your husband to maintain it, and that's the end of it. We don't keep children here, this isn't a nursery. And don't think anyone's going to treat you differently, either.

'No,' Clara says, but *no*'s not big enough to push away the terrible weight she feels accumulating in her body; her *no*'s scarcely a whisper and her will's wimpered away, it's powerless to contradict. Yes, it was that night she told him her secret, that night sealed away in its bubble of pleasure and pain so that she didn't remember it at first. The night Michael betrayed her. The night that's brought her here. No is utterly useless. Everything and everyone is conspiring to destroy her, and it's too much to withstand.

Clara's hands tear and beat at her body. Throwing off the warden who tries to restrain her, she rushes at the cream tiled wall, slamming herself into it as hard as she can. Three times before they stop her she crashes into the wall to kill the child, Michael, herself, the world. It seems this is the last and only thing she can do. But they stop her, one on either arm, one behind: a bleeding nose and a pounding heart the only relief she'll get.

'Co-ee Clara Riley, is that you next door? What's the snivelling for?' disembodied voices sear through the warrened darkness.

'How long've you got, then? You can give us your address – we might need your services after. You better cheer up or it'll seem like forever.'

'What's the matter with her?'

'Been knocked up.'

'Well she ought to know what to do about it!'

Clara wants to tell them, get it straight, but she can't bear to shout into the faceless dark.

'I've had five and I don't know where any of them are.'

'Mine's with my sister, but no one's heard of her for a while. Well what can you do in my line of business?'

'How many've you had, Clara Riley?'

'She's shy.'

'She's gone to sleep, like I'd like to.'

'Silent night
Holy night
All is calm
All is bright – '

Dozens of voices whoop and echo angrily through the words of the carol. Clara, lying in the dark, finds her own lips mouthing the words and her own face screwed in bitter sarcasm as she sings.

'You better learn to be friendly,' says a whisper from the tiny grating at the top of the wall, 'better all round.'

Dr Roberts has been warned. He speaks to Mrs Audley Jones very slowly as if she were deaf. Her silence, he's been told, is pure obstinacy, since she's often heard talking to herself.

'You must miss your home, my dear.'

'You must understand it was a matter of expediency to send you here, the strain you were under would have been too much for a woman of robust constitution, let alone yourself . . .' Dr Roberts coughs into the silence. 'Your husband asks me to tell you he is prepared to engage a companion for you, if you wish to return home. The Admiral feels he ought to have his wife at home, so long as he has one . . .'

Does he really think I'll bargain with him? Think at all?

'. . . would require certain undertakings vis-à-vis your activities and requirements which I as your doctor would, with your own interests at heart, support – '

Doctor! Your soul's soft as a slug, face fat with corruption, a torturer paid by a tyrant, and ignorant, pig ignorant, the lot of you. Any woman'd be better with her grandma's prescription than yours, as free with the knife as you are with the pen and the Hippocratic oath, a 'doctor' registered and regulated by other men such as you, you keep us out of your greasy little freemasonry because we'd find you out and shoo you out, you rat!

Dr Roberts is disconcerted by his patient's appearance of calm indifference. The vaguely philanthropic feelings that swaddled him on his leisurely and well-refreshed journey to Peacehaven are beginning to desert him, leaving behind a stale ache, half hunger, half indigestion. A neat row of tree-tops is just visible from the high barred window, swaying queasily in the wind. Roberts forces himself to look back at Mrs Audley Jones's face.

'That business is all over now, and no blame attached to you; and so we feel a fresh start and a healthy regime . . .'

'What happened?' The question she's asked herself so many times escapes, springing into the room like an apparition. They're both equally startled; Mrs Audley Jones fighting to keep back a torrent of other questions all rushing together, all jostling around the small breach in her months of public silence. She feels as if she is going to choke, waiting while Roberts stammers and fumbles like someone in a room where the lights have been suddenly extinguished.

'Well, er, my dear, so you haven't lost your tongue, now that's hopeful: not much of a life for a woman who can't talk, eh? Well – '

'What happened?'

Dr Roberts is panicking; he feels an overwhelming urge to answer her question but knows the Admiral wouldn't like it. His sense of his own magnanimity has deserted him all at once, and there's a horrible squirming fear, humiliating and consuming, like the feeling in the moment before confessing a childhood misdemeanor.

'Well, my dear, as I said, your name was cleared – ' The woman may be unbalanced, but she's not going to harm me, he reminds himself: but that does no good, that's not where the awful taintedness comes from.

'What happened?'

'Clara Riley's in prison at His Majesty's Pleasure. She

142

pleaded guilty – to attempting to abort herself, and to procuring her own abortion . . . Penfold . . . got off.' The words freeze on his lips. He's told people of their loved ones' imminent deaths with less trouble. He looks at her, and then quickly away, sitting hunched as if prepared for a blow.

'Onward House,' asks Mrs Audley Jones, 'is it still – '

'I believe so,' the doctor replies, smiling in his relief at being the bearer of good news. But Mrs Audley Jones doesn't smile.

'What am I going to do?' she says. Dr Roberts no longer has the presumption to advise. They sit silent in the attic room, each of them alone as the dead weight of their own separate responsibilities settles slowly around their shoulders.

'You should've gone to the woman up the street who'd've kept her mouth shut,' says Lizzie. Clara is standing at the stone sink with the tap running cold and fast scooping up handfuls of water and rushing them to her face, neck, chest, splashing water up her forearms as if the tears are a spreading fire that has taken hold of her and must be extinguished.

'Where was your eyes? There's one on every street. Kept yourselves to yourselves, did you? Well that never pays.'

'She said it was safe.' Being berated has calmed her. Clara plunges her hands into the sink and rests her weight on them, facing the wall.

'Look where safety's got you,' says Lizzie. 'Now don't start the waterworks again. You can't change the past. We all make mistakes. Look at me, I got two years for singing on a bridge. If I'd've known, I'd've sung in my head, wouldn't I? Don't take me wrong, Clara, I'm sorry for you, I really am.'

'And now – ' Clara says, gesturing at herself, 'they keep asking me where he is. He must have gone, I don't know. They want him to pay for it and so do I but it's me they won't leave alone – ' The urge to dash herself against wall, floor, sink, anything hard and obliterating returns, but Clara conquers it: Lizzie's told her that too much of that and you're carted off to the bin in a strait-jacket.

143

'I don't reckon you deserve what you got, Clara, none of us do: we're in here for things we couldn't help. And I'll tell you something, when I get out of here, so long as I'm alive, I'll do what I can to get you out. I'll – someone's coming, come on, let's do this flaming floor . . .'

'Least you'll get some milk to drink,' she whispers, 'and no one's going to try and make you keep the child this time, so why worry?'

Yes, why worry, Clara thinks. I'll have the child and it will be taken somewhere else. That's what I wanted before. Too late. The harsh sound of their brushes scrubbing at stone fills her ears. The floor's as clean as it was yesterday but they scrub and scrub, watched from the door.

Clara gets no applications for visits, no letters, no one enquiring after her. She imagines handing the child to Michael, a bloody screaming bundle. This is what you wanted, she'd say, here. But a man can't raise a child, he'd begin, and she would laugh, laugh, laugh. But of course, he won't come; they're looking for him but how do you find a small quiet man in a city of millions? She's told them again and again she doesn't know where he is, that he was a sick man and out of work, perhaps he's dead – They keep saying she's lying. But they haven't found him. No, she'd said, the next time they asked, he wasn't the father anyway, it was the Prince of Wales, no, it was an immaculate conception, all blue and gold like in church windows. After that they warned her and shut her up in a small cell away from Lizzie and her friend May; she got no milk that week. The milk's watered, but there's still a hint of sweetness to it, a secret warmth like summer dark. Clara drinks it greedily, letting only Lizzie taste. She shines like the pole star in here, Clara thinks of Lizzie, glows like one of Michael's blessed saints. To find such a friend when they've locked you away: it makes her smile, the world's a tangled backwards place, you never find what you want at the time you want or expect it, and nothing's over when you think it is.

144

'Wants to get out, just like the rest of us,' says Lizzie when the child begins to kick. At night, when the kicks come through her dreams and she wakes, wanting to throw open a door and walk, walk until it's day and she's somewhere else, Clara remembers Lizzie's words and finds herself thinking, you'll soon be out and away and free, I'll not be doing you any harm.

Just as she could never quite find the right, meek, little smile for Mrs Rosenbury, Clara can't empty her eyes of dislike when she's spoken to by a wardress.

'You stop acting insolent,' she's told, 'or I'll tell the girls the rest of it. You know what I mean. You killed a baby, a living baby. Even these whores know what to think of that. You kill this one and you'd not live long yourself. One more time you look at me like that and I'll tell them. You'll not be having so many friends sorry for you after that. I'll tell that Lizzie, you understand?'

Clara must hate me, thinks Mrs Audley Jones. I'm here, but I needn't be. She didn't have any choice. Dr Roberts' news and his proposal have gradually taken her over, seeping in through the silence that's petrified thought for so long. Why am I here? she asks herself. I came because I wouldn't betray myself and her and because I was already a prisoner. But I've not stopped them: Clara's in prison and no doubt she thinks I've bought my freedom with hers. What good have I done anyone? The privacy of the asylum is a far cry from the publicity of force-feeding in Holloway. No one knows what I mean, why I'm here, except Olivia and Eleanor, and what can they do? And what could I do even if I was to escape? Once certified, mad for life. What's the use of liberty if you have to hide? I've put myself in a position of complete impotence. Why did I come? she asks again. Out of cowardice? Out of a sense of drama? Did I really have no other choice? Can I sit here in my glass-bowl silence while she scrubs floors in jail? But she can't go back to that house, herself and the companion

145

and the doctor and the Admiral and crowds in the street glimpsed from cab windows and theatre boxes; it would be more of a prison than this. She looks out of the barred window. Far below on the vivid green lawn a group of elderly women take exercise, watched over by three young orderlies, plump, square-standing women from the village nearby. She can hear a trolley of clattering plates being wheeled along the corridor on the floor below. Why did I decide to keep silence, she asks herself? Because I imagined this would go on for ever and self-containment seemed the only way to bear it. Shame fills the small room like a crowd; such a romantic martyrdom, she thinks to herself sarcastically, such a desire for oblivion, such bloody, bloody weakness. As if silence could keep the world frozen harmless, that point of time when, once, her reaction had been appropriate. 'Peacehaven,' she says aloud, slowly, 'is full of people.' Staff who go home each night or on Sundays; some of the patients recover and return to whatever it was that sent them mad, visitors come to see them, as do inspectors once a year. There's scope, much more than in Penley Square with a personal guard. If I try hard enough, and often enough, someone will listen, she thinks. She must begin speaking again, little by little, like taking solids after sickness.

She senses that everything kept at bay by that invisible wall of silence will come back when she begins to talk again. She'll lose her only vestige of an illusion of power and everything will lose its bleached, distant look and become what it is: ugly. Bars are bars. But when a woman with curly hair comes to bring her food, she smiles and says, 'Thank you', just loud enough to be heard.

Clara goes to chapel without protest; Lizzie says it will spoil her chance of earlier release if she makes a point of being a heathen, and besides, if you get a wall-end seat you can have a good talk. They sit in the musky dark with one hymn-book between them and Lizzie turns the pages. When I told Michael it didn't do any good, Clara thinks, her lips moving slow and soundless. Lizzie sings with all her might: she half believes, and besides she's glad of any chance to sing her heart out. Her heart's given her too much trouble, she says; if she could have it out, she would. There's a woman in for poisoning her husband, and one for shooting her father, no one bothers them, Clara thinks, and who they killed were real people with lives, not half-formed things. But then real people might deserve to die, but the newborn and unborn are innocent, that was what people would say. Innocence is like money, Clara thinks . . . She nudges Lizzie, who turns to her, her face flushed into beauty by the singing. Clara's heart begins to hammer at the bones that keep it in. They look down at their book, and Clara has to speak in a steady, dull voice, for whispers carry in church.

'There's something else I did, Lizzie, though that's not what I'm in here for, something different.' Why am I doing this? I don't want to lose a friend. More chance of keeping her if it's me that tells. 'It was nearly twenty years ago.' Lizzie's making tiny nods, but still not turning her head from the book. 'I had a baby girl, and five days after she was born I – ' Lizzie kicks her foot. The church is standing in a minute's silent prayer. Lizzie curls her hands together, and gives them a small but tight and unmistakable twisting movement. Her face impassive, she nods three times. Voices roar out around Clara. The gesture shocked her. Killing, Clara thinks, killing, and shudders. She forgets to move her lips. Lizzie catches her hand briefly as they turn to leave the chapel.

Clara's last birth takes place between dusk and dawn on a summer's night when she has been five months in jail. As before, she finds her body's pain is bearable; indeed, its steady development and sweaty crescendos are almost a comfort in the hot, wakeful night. The women in the cells either side of her are asleep, she can hear their breathing, and hers is scarcely louder than theirs, though it catches differently. This birth is a secret solitaire, part gamble, part dare, a race, chasing her tail hidden in the dark. She wants to bring the child out before it's light and without waking a soul. She bets with herself between breaths that it will be a girl. But the trickiest, secretest game of all that's falling out, luck of the dice, fortune's poxy twisted smile, is that she's betting and begging the child won't be born dead or strangled or ricked in her passages. She doesn't want it snatched away, found dead in a privy, in a box, under a bush, in a cellar, sent away to suckle, never seen again: she wants it for herself.

The chaplain would see this as a triumph of love over fear or sin, and the judge and governor as evidence of the reformatory powers of the penal institution; but, to Clara, as the labour progresses, pressure inside slowly managing to push and puncture its way outwards, it feels strangely as if she's getting back a fragment of what's been taken away, it feels like clutching at not quite empty air. All those things she's wanted. It feels so sad. She knows the newspaper readers would have little pearly tears in their eyes, the Pope would turn unsmiling and say 'God's blessed you, my child, even now' his arms would say, stretching stately lines in the air, so and forever, dew stealing in the very night of hope to bless even the arid desert, the stony ground; they would say this because now she, in prison for the avoidance of motherhood, wants her child. Yet she knows too that it's a defeat to be in this place now, and a defeat to want the child because there's nothing else to want but food and water and bits of soap. A defeat that doesn't bear thinking of; it makes a mockery of all the efforts made before, so much of her life spent avoiding motherhood and dreaming of what's beyond it, now it's come upon her in the night, not like dew, but like strong arms around her, tightening from behind, round the body, pinning the limbs, hand over her mouth just strong enough for there to be the possibility neither of pain nor of struggle. Defeat spreads, velvety like the warmth in muscles loosening after hours of effort, and after it you're changed, like hair gone white overnight.

The floor's not clean, nor the blanket she wears as a shawl. Clara squats with her back against the wall. The tiny square of sky goes grey, the baby's head is out, and neither of them is dead, but everything's wobbling and spewing out on the grey blanket on the floor.

'Lizzie,' Clara calls sharply. She's won, or lost, in any case – 'Lizzie, let them come, I've had it.' Yellow-brown stains on the walls, dark wet of the blanket.

'Lizzie', and then there's a din of bells and shouts. Clara's last and only child is eased from her body, cord cut and tied just as the first yellowness of dawn creeps unwillingly into her cell. The baby girl refuses to cry when she is slapped, but breathes nonetheless.

Clara's taken to rest in the soft bed of the prison hospital. Many admire her baby, but Lizzie's friend May comments drily, 'No wonder she didn't want to fill her lungs with the air in here, any more than we do.'

'Not much for you to see here, is there?' Lizzie says to the child, which searches blindly for Clara's nipple.

The child is called Beth – Beth Riley after Lizzie, the best friend I ever had. Lizzie has points for good conduct, and can see her way out. 'She'd better hang on to that name,' she says, 'it's all she'll ever have. You should've pleaded your belly at the trial.'

'Not with her history,' says May. They laugh, watching as the child feeds; a laugh of mingled strands, some thick and brutal as rope, some thin and cutting as threads, a laugh that takes the place of many contradictory words and expresses a great deal of what they know, but scarcely any mirth. Beth Riley seems a perfect child, untouched by the misery of her environment, her skin and eyes undimmed by her mother's monotonous diet.

'I'd rather have a suck of you than a plate of potato eyes,' says May, 'sweet as anything, mother's milk.'

Beth, with closed eyes, reaches for Clara's breast, hands gentle and unerring as a lover's, sucks soft and steady. Clara feels herself melt inside, though there's an undertow of pain that mounts as the weeks go by.

What will happen to Beth? She will be weaned and then taken away, her mother imprisoned at His Majesty's Pleasure, her father disappeared or dead. She will be as all alone in the world as that little girl collecting autumn leaves from the gutter: if only she'd had something to give then, Clara thinks – and now there's not one promise she could make to Beth and keep.

In the hours between the times when she's allowed to attend to Beth, Clara rehearses the things she wants to tell her, longing to whisper them into the tiny ears that don't understand, but love the tickling of lips and breath, the softness of her voice.

'Beth, you're a kind of miracle, you are.'

'Beth – '

'You didn't ought to let yourself love her so, Clara,' says Lizzie. 'They'll take her away to the orphanage or workhouse or some such, they will.' But Clara turns away, making herself deaf. She won't think of the future, it's unbearable. And she never thinks of the past, all her memories are washed away. Lying on her plank bed at night, she stays awake after the singing's done, dreaming other lives for Beth and herself. She sips her love in secret. Blessing, defeat, victory, comfort, Beth grows and fills her sight entirely.

They believe her now. They never mention Michael.

'God,' says the prison chaplain, 'sends sinful persons many trials, which are opportunities for repentance. My dear, a humble acceptance of His will makes us dear to Him.'

'But it's not right. I want Beth, I love Beth, and now I'm not allowed to keep her – I can't do anything – and all that you said about motherhood was sacred and how what I did was a crime and now – '

'This is a penal institution, not a nursery,' says the warden in charge.

'You're not taking her away.' The pain she's blinded herself to inches towards its crescendo.

'It will be better for the child. If you love her as you say, then you will see that is true. True love is selfless.'

'Your milk is inadequate now. You are not healthy.'

As soon as the child is weaned, she will go.

'I need more to eat, give me just a little more.'

'The diet is in the regulations.'

'Ask the Lord for strength, my daughter, pray.'

Clara spits. But that evening she circles Beth with her arms and she says, and she believes, that they'll never be parted.

'Better the Board than the streets,' says Lizzie, 'and better than that husband of yours from what you've said.'

Clara doesn't answer. There are five days left.

'Couldn't have a little princess like Beth growing up in a mouldy old place like this, now that is a point, Clara . . . oh, what's the use.'

Mrs Audley Jones wears her smile whenever possible. She embroiders samplers and table mats with devotional and floral motifs. 'Thank you,' she says, 'thank you,' to the doctor who comes to inspect the progress of her disease. 'I feel so much better already.' She smiles. She offers to arrange the flowers in the hall. She converses on the subject of the weather. She timidly requests a newspaper, and is given the *Ladies' Fashion Gazette*. She smiles as she accepts it, for the one thing she must not seem is melancholic. She enquires after the children, husband and friends of the woman who brings her food, but then the woman changes, and she has to begin again. And she worries, for how can she change the subject from the weather to paper and pen when the time's ripe. When you've acted for so long, how will people react to the real person? Will they think you're mad or will they trust you?

Outside the walls, the carpet of marsh plants has turned from uniform olive green to scarlet, brown, purple and rust. Dr Roberts visits again; won't she go home? He's heard such good reports – but yes, of course, there would still have to be a companion, just in case.

'Whose good would it serve?' she says, 'I'm not going from one prison to another. You know I shouldn't be here.' Dr Roberts leaves the room immediately, not wanting a repetition of the moral confusion that dogged him after his last visit.

Clara's entrance to the hospital is barred.

'She went this morning. Didn't you say goodbye last night? She went good as gold like she always is – '

In her mind's ear, Clara hears a screaming such as little Beth never yet made, a gasping exhalation of pain and rage amplified and echoing endlessly down the corridors that surround her; she sees the small face all screwed up unrecognisably around its gaping mouth, limbs kicking uselessly in their wrappings.

'Stop that, Riley. Stop it, at once!'

Clara draws shuddering breath, the sound guts her again, and there's a great rolling of boiling stuff behind her eyes.

'And you was the one that didn't want babies, that killed them,' someone shouts.

'I want her, I want her now,' yells Clara, and another great wave, noise become lava, rolls and burns inside her so that she can't hear the reply.

'I want them, I want them, we'll live by the sea, in a house with mahogany, I want them.'

She can see the house, and the children, three of them standing outside the gate, unnaturally bright and clean like in a painting. But their lips move, they're real. A huge door slams in the distance.

She walks towards them. She knows their names. You can see my face in all of them, she thinks, William, Helen and little Beth. We'll go inside, she says, her eyes running along the lines of their faces, we'll go inside and tomorrow we'll go to see what the sea looks like. Beth must be so hungry – she reaches for Beth, but Helen holds her fast. 'What's the matter?' she asks: there's such terror in Helen's eyes. 'What's the matter? It's lovely here, at last we've come.' Helen doesn't answer, but backs against the front door, squeezing the baby to her.

'You killed her,' says William in a voice more like a man's

152

than a boy's. 'And the little one who isn't here, we buried her.'

'Oh no,' says Clara, 'but I didn't mean – ' she takes a step towards Helen, and the screaming begins again.

They sit on the sea-shore eating pieces of yellow cake and the crumbs fall into the sand. The sea makes a noise like cymbals, light dances on it like golden pennies. Beth sleeps on Clara's lap, her face turned up to the sky.

'But you *did*,' Helen is saying, 'you did, you *smothered* me.'

William looks on, unspeaking. Clara feels herself turning to dust inside.

'I didn't know then that everything could be all right. We lived in London in one room that was always wet, and I hadn't any friends, and no money, I didn't know we could be all right; it wasn't you, you were so small you weren't you, I couldn't look after you. Oh Helen, you cried so, it was like you hated the world already, and me as well, I couldn't bear it.'

'She's the only one you wanted,' says Helen, gesturing at Beth. William begins to walk down the beach.

'No, Helen, I just didn't want you then and there. Nor your brother. Beth – '

'Why did you kill me, not him? Because I'm a girl?' The white round of a face looks up at her in stricken hatred.

'Your father wouldn't've let me leave you with – '

'Where is he? Where is he?'

'And where is my father?' asks William, suddenly returned and standing close, casting a long shadow on the sand.

The house has electric lights and an electric iron much lighter than the old-fashioned type. Clara stands at her ironing board in the front parlour with the shutters and velvet curtains drawn, ironing the children's clothes. Her eyes stray to the luxuries and elegance that surround her, her fingers taste and taste again the quality of her children's clothes, but she never wonders where it all comes from. Her iron, shiny steel and clean as a whistle, presses linen to marble smoothness. She begins on the lace frill around Helen's nightdress, pushing

153

the point of the iron up into the tiny folds. 'If only they could forget,' she says aloud, 'if only they could forget, everything would be perfect.' The frill turns brown, then black before her eyes, puffing up dirty-smelling smoke. Of course she can't forget I killed her. I put the pillow over her head and waited, I breathed a sigh of relief when it was done, oh what a monster I am, oh Helen. What a weak and evil woman, that I couldn't manage somehow. Lots of women have a flock of babes, Michael said, and still smile the whole day through; lots of people have less of a wage than me but bring up their kids in the ways of God. But not me. I killed Helen. I couldn't bear the thought. I wanted somewhere like this for us, and now it's too late, because I killed Helen. Would we be here if I hadn't? And what about the operation? They all know that too. I can't pretend. They're all here despite me. I've burnt her nightdress, yesterday I dropped her plate. The boy is watching me, watching me watching her all the time, he won't let her forgive me. Forgive? How could she? Would I? She'll only do it because she's no choice. It won't be free, if it's at all. I killed her. Poor little thing, with my face but small and Michael's half-red hair. But she didn't look like that then. What did she look like? I can't even remember, did I ever look? She wasn't Helen then. No face, no name, just a fact, and a scream. Perhaps she knew before I did, perhaps that's why she screamed. Perhaps there's a God. What wouldn't I do to change it now. If I'd been born someone else. They never punished me for it: it is its own punishment, they said, and I didn't really know what they meant. Then they took Beth away. Then they gave them all back, but they all hate me for what I did to them. I never knew I'd see them again. Oh what a world. Oh what a house. But it's a dream. What I did before was in another kind of world. You can't compare, because all the ifs and buts are different. This is a dream.

But the children, she remembers, felt solid enough and warm as she took them upstairs to bed, the pile of clothes she's washed were creased and grimy.

It was wrong, wrong, wrong. They should've punished me.

But what would that have done? The tiny breathing just tussled a bit and stopped . . . The boy's been all right, he speaks like a lord, like a judge – 'It was the idea of you all, not you,' she shouts aloud. The house waits a few seconds, and then the answer comes: a slow whimpering from Helen and Beth's room, it's Helen crying in her sleep. She hears doors eased open and shut, knows William has gone into the girls' room, but the crying doesn't stop, there's no sound of voices soothing or comforting, they're waiting up there, just waiting. 'Stop,' she whispers, 'please stop, oh Helen stop, there's nothing to be afraid of now.' As if in answer the crying redoubles, the crying of someone mangled and maimed and alone in the dark, its intensity increasing minute by minute, until a terrible thing begins to happen –

'Stop it, damn you,' growls Clara, and finds herself slowly making for the door, flooded by that awful single-minded desire to obliterate the source of the noise..

'No,' she tells herself, 'no', but her hand pushes down the handle, opens the door. The crying's suddenly louder now the heavy door's open. 'No', she shuts her eyes and stands still. 'I'll die instead. Stand here until it kills me.'

William appears on the landing, holding Beth. 'Mother,' he calls, 'please come up and see to Helen.'

For a second there's silence, even Helen's quiet, all waiting.

'I – just – can't,' gasps Clara, even as she tries to deny her own words, struggles to take the first step, but she can't, and the crying begins anew, announcing failure.

Slowly one of the strangers becomes recognisable, and a sound attaches to her lips.

'Now, why the waterworks, Clara? Don't you know me? It's Lizzie.'

The two worlds pull at Clara, now one, now the other seems the stronger, but neither is attractive. Lizzie bends over and pushes Clara's damp hair from her face.

'Come on,' she says. 'It's Lizzie, I can't stay long.'

And Clara grasps Lizzie's hand to save herself from the

155

children, brown now from the sun and living in the house like frightened wily animals, disappearing at the sound of her footsteps, snarling and weeping if she catches them or touches them, running into the sea and playing drowned, laughing at her tears, sounds from the rooms at night, the creak of footsteps, soft voices when Helen's nightmare is done – She grasps Lizzie's hand.

'They all hate me for what I did, and there's nothing I can do, they're going to kill me in the end because what I did was murder – '

'Now Clara, you're talking about your nightmares, but you've woke up now, you've had bad dreams because you've had a bad life that's made you do bad things, but it's only nightmares. It's the good in you judging on the bad when you're asleep. Now don't you get the two muddled up, or you'll be no better than any drunken annie.'

'I have nightmares too, but they don't last a month,' says the other woman, who is May. 'Then you are the one that likes to do things in style – '

Lizzie interrupts: 'Clara, I'm getting out. And I'm a woman of my word, remember my promise? I'll do my best for you – '

'Can't you have Beth, can't you take Beth?' says Clara. Lizzie shakes her head.

'No. They wouldn't let me and I couldn't anyway.' Clara turns away.

'Now Clara, you ought to be glad for me. I'll visit you. And May here's going to look after you for me.'

'And the first thing,' says May, 'is keep your mouth shut about those nightmares, or you'll end up some place worse than this and stay there till you die.'

'If there's a war, it'll be the breaking of us,' Miss Handley mutters to Alice Toms as she prepares to mount the box after the woman speaking about trade unions. A rough, hot wind snatches at words and clothing alike but the Corner is more crowded than usual, as though rumours of war have sent people looking for new formulations of truth. Alice Toms has

156

been growing three inches a year, and now stands a head above Miss Handley, broad-shouldered and solemn-looking.

'And *they*'ll let us down as well,' continues Miss Handley. 'I don't know why she bothers. Yes, everyone'll be out waving flags and marrying heroes, sending white feathers and crying for the dead. Plenty for women to do in a war, there always is. I don't suppose you remember the last one?'

'No,' says Alice, 'perhaps . . .'

'Oh, we might even get the vote out of it in the end. But it'll do for us, just the same.'

'Now in this country, we pride ourselves on being free,' begins Miss Handley, and she's answered by cheers, disconcertingly loud and edged with hysteria. 'But I'd like to talk to you today about the chains that bind woman and the prison she lives in, sometimes literally. Now one of our chains is the bearing of children, or to put it another way the lusts of men, or to put it yet another way, unregulated fertility . . .'

Alice thinks she recognises a constable on the edge of the crowd and wills Miss Handley not to go too far, not to mention the words 'preventative measures' nor promise to distribute the 'simply worded leaflet' that's already had Miss Wise in court.

'I know of a woman,' Miss Handley is saying, 'who has been incarcerated in prison for attempting to rid herself of an unborn child, and another woman who – ' The crowd hisses, like a hostile army straightens its back.

'Shame!' shouts one man, the others wait –

'Had she other means,' Miss Handley shouts above the rising noise of the crowd, 'she would not have had to resort to such dangerous and repugnant methods. And other means are available. It's only prejudice and oppression that prevent their distribution and use. How many women would seek, if only they were allowed, even enjoined to – '

Alice slips into the crowd, the roll of leaflets in her pocket. She examines faces, trying to decide who would be grateful for instruction on the regulation of fertility, and who would consider it obscene. Some of the crowd, perhaps three or four, will have come hoping for a leaflet. A small woman, still half girl, catches her eye, nods, accepts the paper and smuggles it up her sleeve.

'I call you lot the angels of deliverance,' she says, following Alice as she works her way to the outside of the crowd. 'What we want next is something to make 'em want to sleep at night like the rest of us.'

'. . . not new knowledge, not a modern invention, this is knowledge that has been deliberately suppressed.' Miss Handley's voice fades as the two women walk away.

'Great Britain is straining, like the great bulldog we are, straining at the leash of politicians' cowardice. Great Britain wants war, and she wants victory. The Kaiser –'

'Drunk,' says Alice Toms loudly as they pass the speaker, a man in a faded suit gesturing wildly and spitting as he speaks.

'Women may sneer, but they don't know what battle is. They don't care what way the world goes, only so long as they can buy new hats and go to shameless dances . . . but we men know, we know what we have to do, and we do it for them as well, and for their children. War, that's what.' Her companion steers Alice away.

'Look,' she says, 'there's that man again', gesturing at a pale, sandy-haired man sitting silent between two speakers, placards propped on either side of him. 'Suffering is the path to grace', one says; the other declares, 'The Lord is our Judge'. One of his eyes is sealed over with gathered folds of wine-coloured skin, the other follows them as they pass him by.

'Afternoon,' mumbles Alice. 'Looks so sad, doesn't he?'

'They use this kind of place for prisoners of war. Just imagine, one of the wings cleared out and filled with young soldiers kicking their heels, the other full of mad women, oh pardon me, Mrs Audley Jones, I do count you apart from the rest of them.'

'Have you got a young man, Jenny?' asks Mrs Audley Jones, a sweet girl, she thinks, full of life even in a place like this.

158

'Well,' says Jenny, lingering with the tray, 'in a manner of speaking. There's a young man from Durham who writes to me. But – I'll tell you a secret, I've not met him yet, because I answered an advertisement in the *Gazette*. "Lonely young man", it said, "seeks thoughtful young woman to exchange correspondence and forge a lasting friendship . . ." and so I answered it.' Jenny laughs as she picks up the tray. She'll get married soon, thinks Mrs Audley Jones. Lasting friendship. She'll get stouter after each child and she'll go on laughing but her eyes will have a betrayed look about them. Look what you did for Clara, replies a voice in her head.

'Letters,' says Mrs Audley Jones, just as Jenny reaches the door, 'I'd so like to write a letter. Jenny, you wouldn't help me – '

'Mrs Audley Jones! You didn't ought to ask. You shouldn't ask me to risk my prospects,' says Jenny, almost angry. 'You probably don't know what it means but I have to work for my living, and don't you ask me that again.'

But I'll have to, Jenny, thinks Mrs Audley Jones, I'll have to.

'This great country needs everyone,' the prison governor thunders. 'This island has been called a jewel set in a sparkling sea; we have riches and we have civilisation and a powerhouse of industry second to none. And the people of these islands have a sense of right and religion and know when to fight for it.' He is a major, retired from active service, a small but broad man with flushed skin erupting above his stiff white collar. Today, 5 August 1914, he wears his medals pinned to his suit. He stands behind his claw-footed table, its uncluttered surface polished to an almost unbearable shine that catches the eye and hurts it like sunshine on metal. Behind him sit those few of the trustees who have nothing better to do on this second day of war: the ladies and the chaplain. His hands tucked behind him, he addresses seventy-five women prisoners. 'A just war can be man's finest hour,' he continues, 'a woman's too, and even yours. For it offers an opportunity for service,

159

service willingly dedicated to a higher cause.' The atmosphere is sullen.

'If people's locked up, you can't tell how willing they is or isn't,' shouts May, and though Clara catches her eye and smiles at her before she's taken out swearing, 'filthy hypocrite buggers', her heart sickens with the pointlessness of May's defiance. In prison nothing can have the result it ought, it's all stifled. Even her own prison loves for Beth and Lizzie have had this quality: like the pitted potatoes grown and dug by the prisoners, they provide some but not enough nourishment; some, but still insufficient pleasure; they're marked by the soil they grew in, the grudges that tended them, they're provisional, and they're snatched away.

The governor speaks louder now, and with less poetry. 'For those of you who answer our country's demand, there's an opportunity to go some way to blotting out the moral debt your past behaviour has put you in. As for those of you who do not wish to do so, the debt is still there: young men will die to defend you, just as the innocent are defended, and, indeed, your debt, and shame, will increase. I shall see to it that, willingly or unwillingly, you go some way to paying the material part of that debt.' His passion finds no echo in the silent, resentful gathering. Clearly angry, he continues, 'Those with good behaviour and no evidence of violence on their records will be escorted to work in the munitions factory. Those left will work harder on the land. Food may well be scarce . . .' After dark they will sew kit-bags and roll bandages. Fuel will be rationed. Clara lies on her plank bed listening until all the whispers and cat calls have reached their nightly crescendo. There's no call from May, locked up in punishment, where no sounds reach. A couple of voices call 'Clara, Clara' but she lies without answering as they gradually squabble into silence.

Will she be going into munitions or staying? She'd rather stay. The hurt of the last war scarcely touched her, it being so far away and a volunteer's war, Michael too old to serve in any case. Now she's locked up mercifully away from this one, digging potatoes and sewing, nothing left to lose, no pleasures, no money, no freedom, no loved one sent away to die. Even so, something like a premonition touches her, a half-heard whispering, an almost-seen image that freezes the blood: war. Clara has a terrible sense of countless last breaths exhaled all at once, and again, again: the moment's vision repeats and repeats, won't stop. Clara clutches the thin gritty blanket. The full glare of moonlight has thrust its way into the cell, an ammoniac light, strong and sickly as the smell of piss that she's never grown used to. War. An occasional whinnying clatter punctuates the quiet outside, as if odd scraps of a wind had been left behind during the day. Clara's wide awake, oh so wide awake, despite the hard day's work she's done; she thinks, as she does nearly every night, of her never-never children who have grown unseen between these prison walls. A boy, a girl and baby Beth, now standing upright and almost steady. She sees them all at once, their different ages, their faces smiling then sad, like the passing of the seasons that has made them older. The boy, William, is a man now, off to the front, he's old enough. The girl she couldn't comfort, condemned to scrimp and suffer in the shadow of war, and baby Beth – who knows? A prison baby that wouldn't cry, a late baby, loved and snatched away, her hair like a crown of gold, her face still smiling: they're all she has, these pictures. There's something in all the children's faces that must've come from her.

Three lives come out of her to be mashed and grinded in the swirl and blunder of history. These are no times for the bearing of children, no times at all. Where are they? Where are they? At least one's dead and buried. Yes, she's killed even before there was a war; maybe she's bad, maybe there's too many bad like her and that's why there's a war – come like the plague. But those that kill in the war will be called heroes. They will be defending something. What can she say but that something drove her to it, and it felt at the time more like stopping something bad than doing bad; it felt like she was defending something too. And it could have been otherwise and it felt different from this terrible rasp of a whisper of the beginning of a war. What's done is done, dreams would be different and she can tell some things are right or wrong or, at least, better or worse than others, even though people have acted like she was a monster and called her a dangerous and unnatural woman, even though they spat at her from the gallery and no one but Lizzie and May will really listen. She knows the war is a bad thing, far worse than anything she ever did, knows from her heart it will be loss, nothing but loss. And long after it's over, the losses will be piled up behind everyone, the guiltiness. I know, she thinks, I know. A sudden, acute anger like physical pain pulls her head down on to her knees. She wants to spit the world out. She feels both weakened and exalted by the strength of her feelings, and by a sudden understanding, clear but wordless like a painting or a symbol, of herself Clara Riley, in the prison, in the world, a woman.

The moment passes into silence, listening. Clara wishes for the rushing of a good strong wind, a drying wind, the kind that blows the creases right out, a billowing, billowing raging wind to make everything good as new. She feels for a moment beyond loss, she wants to be free; she wants to be that wind.

Coming out of mass, Michael stops suddenly in his tracks. There's a woman sitting on the stone bench at the bottom of the steps, her back to him. She's wearing a coat with a fox-fur collar and sitting very upright, her hands resting in her lap. Clara. But the next moment he knows it isn't. He walks slowly down the steps and past the woman without turning to look.

Michael passes most of his days alone, tending lawns and ornamental flowerbeds in new streets where the houses are large, but not large enough to warrant a full-time gardener. The evenings he spends in a room smaller even than any they ever shared, with his bible or prayer book on his lap, sometimes copying texts in large letters on to sheets of brown wrapping paper. But tonight, he thinks of Clara. In the blinking of an eye her presence fills the room, obliterating the texts nailed to the walls, and then vanishes, leaving behind it a great ache of love and loneliness. Clara, as she would stand sometimes at the table, her hands busy, her eyes staring straight ahead, her face softened by dreams he could only guess at. Clara, shaking her head slowly, deliberately: she won't come to mass. Clara, as she covered his good eye and brought the candle close – oh Lord, she fills the room like a ghost.

He lights the gas. I lost her because the church was locked, he thinks. No, that's not it – He has no proper white paper, so carefully cuts the fly-leaf from a book of sermons, then writes his address in the flowing copperplate learned all those years ago in the Evening Institute.

Dear Clara, If there is anything I can do –

The thick ink dries to a purplish sheen in the heat of the lamp. He doesn't know where to begin. The words come as hard as forgiveness has. How will he address the letter; where is she? She stood in court and she said something about 'my husband' but he never heard what she said.

'Let's go over the other bridge,' says Lizzie to Cherry, 'this one has bad memories for me. This dress'll have to go – who'd've thought the styles would've changed so much? But I always liked the colour.'

'Looks better in electric light,' says Cherry. 'Can't say the same for my face.'

'You do look older, then I suppose I do as well.'

'I had a baby for my sins. Takes it out of you. Died. Pity, it was ever such a pretty little thing and good as gold. There you go. I had to work, didn't I? I've got a real thirst, why don't we drop in here, Lizzie, and you can tell me about – '

'No, Cherry, let's go on a bit further, let's go along beside the river, here, look – ' She wants to keep out of the familiar; once she's settled into it she feels that will be the end, she'll never do any different, and she'll forget about her promises to Clara and herself . . . She can feel Cherry's unwilling, pulling-

163

back and fuddling her sense of purpose, like a warm bed on a winter morning.

'Cherry, I don't want to go back to that kind of work, it'd do for me in the end, and you as well, look at us – ' The two women pause to peer at themselves in a dark pane of glass, arm in arm they stand, their faces almost blank with the light catching the tops of their curls.

'What's the matter with you? Met a nice handsome priest in there or something?'

'I don't mean it's wrong what we do, it's just not doing us any good, is it?'

Cherry laughs scornfully, stopping abruptly to ask, 'So what else can we do? Go and help some lout clip sheep in Australia? Meet a Duke in the park and marry him?'

'And there's Clara. She's in there on His Majesty's Pleasure for having her insides cleared out, would you believe it. It's a long story, Cherry, but I promised I'd try to get her out – '

'What d'you promise a thing like that for? Never make promises is what I say.'

'She had a baby and they took it away from her, she called it Beth after me. Oh Cherry, I don't know how to go about it all, but sure as hell, on my back in the upstairs of the Albert isn't the place to start.'

'There's a war on, in case you forgot,' says Cherry. 'What's the matter with you for heaven's sake? You were always soft, but – '

'You don't have to come along with me, I'm just telling you what I've made up my mind about.'

They stop at a small retaining wall and look down into the water. The sun is very low, and their side of the river is in deep shadow. Logs and bubbles toss on the narrow shore, to their left the river opens up into a swathe of gold.

'It took me a good while to find you, but I wanted to because I thought you just might want to help me, Cherry. But if you don't – ' Lizzie leaves her sentence incomplete. The tide's still rising and the water slaps fitfully at a row of cracked posts just visible above its surface.

'I've heard of a place where they teach whores typing and put them up till they've got somewhere to go . . . Onward House, I think it's called, been going a few years now,' says Cherry. 'That might be a good start, though what it does for your Clara I couldn't say . . . We could go there, if that's the sort of thing you mean.'

Lizzie nods. 'I've heard of it,' is all she says, squeezing Cherry's arm.

Other new fiction from Virago

BACK IN THE FIRST PERSON
Kathy Page

A slap in the face – Cath's face – is, according to Steve, 'no big deal'. But to Cath it's the final straw: she tells him to get out. He returns to rape her – 'I think you owe it to me'. In the months which follow, Cath is to discover that rape is considered not a very serious matter. Police incredulity, medical callousness, legal delays, and finally courtroom theatrics – all obscure the truth, almost from Cath herself. Caught between her own tenuous self-control and unadmitted need to tell what has happened and be believed, she becomes walled up in her own silence. Yet in this painful year of cross-examination and self-examination, Cath is finally able to move back into the first person, taking charge of her life once more.

In this impressive first novel, Kathy Page writes with great courage about the far-reaching consequences of a particular kind of violence.

Other new fiction from Virago

JUMPING THE CRACKS
Rebecca O'Rourke

Nearly midnight in London's derelict Hackney on a wet, windy, dark night, but not so dark that Rats (after her rats' tail hair) doesn't see the Rolls with the body slumped inside. No phone boxes work, no one else on the street: so she clutches her hideous secret and makes for home.

In the days and months that follow, Rats experiences the city with increasing menace – as though existing on the margins, a lesbian, 'unlucky in love', unemployed, a northerner, living alone at the mercy of unscrupulous landlords weren't bad enough. And her job, when she finally lands one, is more evidence of a city in decay – a seedy accommodation agency, teetering on the edge of legality. In her waking and dreaming hours, fraud, corruption and the murder glide ever nearer, as silent and threatening as the hovering Rolls, but she fights them all. Even the return of her lover, Helen, doesn't divert her from her obsessive attempts to track down the killer. Politics and crime, love and loneliness, the search for origins and understanding combine together in this impressive and gripping first novel.

Other new fiction from Virago

NO WORD FROM WINIFRED
Amanda Cross

Once more Kate Fansler, Professor of English and part-time detective, is called from academic life to investigate an unsolved disappearance. Winifred Ashby, honorary niece of Charlotte Stanton, principal of an Oxford college and popular novelist, leaves the seclusion of a New England farm for London to meet Charlie Lucas, whom she has approved as official biographer of her 'aunt'. But, after one informative meeting with Charlie, Winifred mysteriously vanishes. Armed only with Winifred's enigmatic journal, Charlotte Stanton's novels and a piece of folded plastic with a pin in the back, Kate must use her intuition and intelligence to follow a meagre trail which leads from Oxford to a Modern Languages Association convention in New York, to Santa Cruz and, finally, to the unravelling of Winifred's secret past. Can her baffling disappearance mean, as Kate feels in her bones, that she is dead? And, if not, why has there been no word from Winifred? Playing with the lives of three literary women – Dorothy L. Sayers, Mary Renault and Muriel St Clare Byrne – this highly entertaining novel subtly explores the riddles of friendship, inheritance, illegitimacy and passion.

Other new fiction from Virago

YOU CAN'T GET LOST IN CAPE TOWN
Zoë Wicomb

Frieda Shenton has returned to South Africa, a reluctant visitor to the country from which, as a young woman, she sought escape. She has put behind her the childhood years in rural Namaqualand and later experiences of living and working in Cape Town: there was no reconciling the restrictions of apartheid and her father's vision of what her own bright potential might mean for his family and his people – 'We'll show them, Frieda, we will . . . Brains are for making money.' Frieda knew that education, for a Black woman, meant neither freedom nor an end to personal insecurity. But now, years later, return brings a fresh perspective, not a vindication of her exile. Visiting family, talking with friends, in fleeting glimpses of the clandestine resistance movement, Frieda must confront the ambiguities of her exclusion and acknowledge the price of having strayed from the culture that shaped her.

Zoë Wicomb's first collection of connected stories is a superb portrayal of a woman coming to terms with her rejected racial inheritance. Marvellously vivid in their recreation of past experience and in their fine pinpointing of the present, the stories intertwine as incidents recalled build upon each other to give shape to Frieda's identity.

Other new fiction from Virago

THE CENTURY'S DAUGHTER
Pat Barker

The Century's Daughter is Pat Barker's most brilliant achievement yet – the story of a northern working-class community seen through the eyes of Liza Jarrett, born on the last stroke of midnight as the twentieth century begins. Liza never forgets her mother's humiliation in the steel magnate's house where she cleans: her childhood teaches her much about loyalty, love and fortitude. Growing up in the First World War, she married Frank – mystic, faith healer and unemployed steel worker – and, supported by neighbours and friends, brings up her children through the hardship of the Depression. The Second World War brings the greatest trial of Liza's strength, but she survives, humour intact, into the sixties and seventies, caring for her beloved granddaughter Kath, only to see 'progress' do what the Depression and war failed to do: break the community which nourished her.

This is also Stephen's story, the tale of a young community worker alienated by education and homosexuality from parents he can now hardly talk to and a job he bitterly defines as finding ways for the unemployed to pass their time. Stephen comes to Liza to offer help, but stays instead to be helped.

A remarkable mixture of naturalistic style and poetic sensibility, this outstanding novel captures flawlessly the taut, hard humour and warmth of people who have had short shrift both in literature and in life.